ESSENCE REDEEMED

ESSENCE EXTRACTED BOOK THREE

CAREY DECEVITO

DEDICATION

For those who continue to persevere no matter how dark
the outlook may be.

ACKNOWLEDGMENTS

I can't believe this is the end of another series.

A book may write itself in a day, but that's just the beginning. So many people are involved in bringing forth the best of the best to keep you readers entertained; and entertained I hope we have.

First of all, the Essence Extracted trilogy would have never happened had it not been for Nick and Kim. Without that proverbial kick in my ass—years in the making to boot—I would have never made the leap it took to bring Payton and Rafe to life.

Clarise, my beautiful friend from the other side of the world, and my gifted cover designer. Your vision for EE's covers was impeccable.

Karen and Joanne, without you two, I'd have nothing but an inconsistent jumble of words tarnished. Thanks to you two ladies, you've made Payton and Rafe sparkle as they should.

And most importantly, you wonderful readers, bloggers, and fellow authors. Without your support and your push, sometimes I'd still be writing, but I doubt I'd have as much fun doing it as I have been. Enjoy the end of Payton and Rafe's journey!

CHAPTER 1

RAFE

It had been a week since Payton's rescue and no major incident had occurred. Although relieved at the lack of eventfulness, everyone knew it was a matter of time before hell and fire would come raining down on us all. The Fae people were on pins and needles; the tension in the air so thick one could cut it with a knife.

Over the last few days, Mom and Dad had brought my match and me up to speed on the royal family's history—Payton's history. I could see the woman's confidence in what she stood for bloom before my very eyes, and that went a long way to assuage my rising anxiety. I was able to focus on a plan of action for what would come next.

Also, word had spread throughout the Fae people that a royal was within their midst, thus shaking things up since they all believed the bloodline had been nothing more than extinct.

Payton's abilities had grown in potency too, despite her seeing them as useless. It hadn't taken my father and me long to reassure her everything would come together smoothly and much quicker if she didn't suppress her gifts—they did serve a purpose, no matter how minimal they may seem to her. She remained objective about it all, even going through the motions to use them at the most inopportune of times. I'll never forget the blush that spread on my father's face while she sent me pleasurable images through our mind link a few days ago. It resulted in me realizing I needed to get a hold on my own abilities; learn how to build a wall between those I didn't want to share my thoughts with, until I decided I needed to. Payton's gift of command had been a hoot to watch improve. The woman had my brothers twisted like pretzels and at her beck and call. Those two, despite their attempts at resisting her 'persuasive' ways, couldn't help but indulge her whims. I put a stop to it, however, when Andrew showed up with her favorite brand of ice cream last night, citing it was my duty to indulge those desires for her, all the while indulging in her icy treat at her side.

The hardest thing for me though was the limitation of physical intimacy I was able to allow myself with my match, due to the events of a week ago.

Don't get me wrong, I wanted nothing more than to sink balls deep into her snug, hot body, but my head kept me at a distance.

I knew Payton was more than ready to explore us sexually. If her mind link scenarios hadn't been clear enough, the fact she'd voiced it, as recently as last night was proof positive. I just didn't want her to rush things. She might have been fine while she was awake, but her subconscious spoke volumes to the trauma she'd suffered at Matt's hands. With each night, her night terrors weren't showing any sign of easing or disappearing altogether. To be honest, I had a slight inkling I wasn't quite ready either. My mind was still reeling with thoughts of inadequacy, reliving my worst thoughts, and the events leading up to my match's rescue as if on a timeless loop. It had been hell.

PAYTON

I love lazy Saturdays.

Nothing beats the warmth of being cocooned under piles of fluffy blankets, the silence, the comfort in feeling safe, or being so relaxed your body just melts into the mattress with the sense of no cares.

Nothing…except for having a set of strong arms wrapped around you, adding exponentially to the allure of safety.

Shifting carefully to avoid waking Rafe, I settled back in, my head tucked on his chest, under his chin, with one arm draped over his torso. I breathed in the scent of soap and man, the mix never failing to make my heart race, my hormones shifting into overdrive.

It had been over a week, and despite Matt's attempts that horrified me to no end, my blood still boiled for the man lying next to me.

Despite the dark thoughts floating around in my head, my hand began to trace over my match's chest, smoothing over the sparse hair there, down to his navel, across that treasure trail which always led to such a promise of pleasure, toward…

"What are you doing?"

His rough and sleepy baritone had me wanting to jump him.

"Exploring." I kissed his chin, then pushed all things dark out of my mind, my urges to debauch my match far too strong to ignore.

For once, he let me.

Then he didn't.

"S-stop," he said, sounding as if he were in pain.

I never thought I'd beg for him to just let me make him feel good, but there was always a first. "Please."

"Pay…" his voice trailed as my hand proceeded further south, tickling his treasure trail, then continued to sneak past the elastic of his boxer briefs.

"Let me," I urged at a whisper, feeling his body respond to my touch, yet I could tell by the ticking of his jaw and tension in his brow, something wasn't right.

In the next second, his hand reached for my questing wrist in a bruising hold, wrenching it from his body and throwing it back at me as though it was offensive, then his body jackknifed up and out of bed. His breathing was ragged, fury shone in his gaze.

"I asked you to stop," he growled.

I knew he'd never hurt me for anything, but it didn't help the sense of panic that hit me in the moment, causing me to back up, cowering against the headboard, the blankets pulled up to my neck with my knees hitched at my chest.

"Rafe," my voice shook.

"How dare you," he yelled. "You have no clue what I've been through, do you?"

I knew he had issues that spanned from Matt kidnapping me, but it wasn't until now I realized he had his own set of demons he was battling—demons we should have discussed much earlier than before this explosion.

I felt shamed at not seeing it coming. For someone who was so attuned with others' emotions, I'd failed epically. I'd neglected to see that I hadn't been the only one to suffer through my latest ordeal alone.

I was a jerk.

The biggest.

Putting my fear to the side, I made my approach known as I slowly crawled to his side of the bed, grabbed his hands, and looked him in the eye.

"Tell me."

RAFE

Tell me.

Her words resonated in my mind.

We hadn't discussed much more than the basic happenings of Payton's kidnapping, never delving into the emotional side of things since her rescue, or even what I'd done to get to her. Maybe that's what was blocking me—us—from being who we were before the events that nearly had me lose her.

I decided right then, as her cold, clammy hands held mine, I'd talk…then it would be her turn.

Clearing my throat from the large lump threatening to choke me, I started.

"I could hear you calling my name, pleading with me to open my eyes," I swallowed, "but I couldn't wake up no matter how hard I tried."

As if I'd been transported back to the scene of the crash, I could smell smoke and the all too pungent scent of fuel in the air. It had rendered my breathing increasingly difficult, and my head pounded from the hit that had knocked me out cold moments earlier.

"You shrieked out in pain, then glass scattered everywhere. When I opened my eyes, they'd already had you shoved inside the back of their car." I closed my eyes, trying to shake the vividness of the memories away. "Our eyes met, but I couldn't move. I watched as one of the guys hit you over the head with the butt of his gun." My stomach roiled. "They drove off with you, and I couldn't do a thing to stop them until rage had me so consumed for revenge, I finally got my thumb out of my ass and figured out how to free myself. I dragged my ass out of the wreckage and waited for help."

Payton's hand came up to cradle my cheek and I

accepted the comfort. Thank fuck she was safe now.

Her simple gesture gave me the fortitude to continue.

"I lay in the grass for God knows how long when my brothers and father showed up. Had you not thought to call from my phone, I doubt anyone would have come looking as soon as they did." I remember my father asking me where Payton was, the panic overwhelming me about what they were doing to her, every scenario getting darker as they came to mind. "I made a vow, as Patrick and Andrew helped carry me to Dad's car, I'd find my way to get you back, even if it killed me."

"Rafe…"

"My soul ached so much without knowing what was going on with you, I barely slept a wink that first night. I know what it's like to be alone, but I never really knew until I was faced with the possibility of never seeing you…never being with you again," I told her. "We have a life to build together, and the thought of never having it happen only strengthened my resolve to get to you quicker."

Payton's face was pale, tears streaming down her cheeks, but I held steadfast. I was afraid if I pulled her to me like I wanted to, the story would come to a halt, and we wouldn't be anywhere near reaching a resolution to this stalemate I'd imposed on our physical intimacy.

"I must have dozed off sometime during that first night, but something woke me up. I could have sworn I'd heard your voice." I took a deep breath. "I thought it had been a nightmare, then I looked over and noticed you weren't anywhere to be found. And that's when I heard it again…your sweet voice."

"I called out to you a few times after I woke up in that room," she said.

"I'm sorry." I squeezed her hands in mine. "I completely forgot to focus on our mind link. Maybe if I'd done that sooner, then—"

"No!" She pulled her hands from my grip and grabbed both sides of my neck, her eyes never leaving mine. "You had your own set of injuries to deal with. Don't you dare blame yourself."

"It took me calling out to you five times before you finally heard me."

"I heard you before then, but I didn't believe it at first."

"When I finally realized we were linked, I need you to know, I did everything to get to you," my voice grew sturdier as I went on. "I would have torn this entire town apart had Kristie not shown up on our doorstep."

"My watcher, my savior…my man," she whispered, then kissed the side of my mouth before letting my face go to grab hold of my hands again.

Finally realizing she was still kneeling before me on the mattress and I was still standing, I made to sit at her side; then shuffled her so she sat across my lap.

"This tiny woman showed up, bruised cheek and blackened eye, worry and panic crossed over her features and tight posture, and I knew…I knew, Payton, we'd found you." I squeezed her tight. "You were under our noses all that time, in the Davis house. I should have known with their depravity, they'd have some sort of secret dungeon on their property."

"Then you came," Payton said, holding on to me for all she was worth.

"I did," I growled. I'd hated the state I found her in. Tied up and helpless to defend herself, bruised and bandaged. "It hurt to see what he'd done to you."

"Superficial, Rafe."

"Your nightmares tell me otherwise."

"I'll get over it."

I told her what Mom and Dad had talked to me about a few days ago when I'd mentioned her night terrors. "You need help."

Turning her head so our gazes connected, her eyes shone with conviction. "All I need is you."

"Can you forgive me?"

Her brows knitted together. "For what?"

"For the accident. For not coming for you sooner. For–" God, I hope she still loved me, that there was really a way past this for us.

"Shut the fuck up!"

I did as she asked, feeling the surge of power come off of her in waves.

"I love you, Rafe. You." She latched on to my shoulders. "There's nothing to forgive. There will be more attacks on my life, I'm sure of it." Cue my growl, despite my knowing she spoke the truth. "But I know if something happens where I'm taken away, you and your family won't quit until you find me. No matter what, know I'll do everything in my power to make sure I find my way back to you. We're stronger together and growing even more with each passing day. If the likes of the Davis clan can't keep us apart, then we can overcome anything."

"Pay–"

"No, listen to me. I was beaten, I was violated physically, but I wasn't raped, Rafe. I didn't give Matt anything I wasn't ready to deal with, despite what it might have looked like."

That's when I couldn't help myself. Grabbing her face in my hands, I crashed my lips onto hers in a searing kiss. Just like that, with her little tangent, she eased every single fear and anxiety I'd been holding onto since the night she was taken.

CHAPTER 2

PAYTON

A second week had come and gone since my abduction. I've always been the impulsive one; the one who acted out first and not always being successful with my end results either.

With that said, I met with multiple influential people in the Fae world too, noting they were all on our side. None of the heads from the other factions had been willing to discuss a peaceful end to this quarrel, which had been going on for centuries. As pointless as it ended up being, I knew I had to at least try. It seemed like no matter how valiant our attempts at a peaceful outcome were, we found ourselves slowly inching toward this war everyone's thoughts had been consumed by. The proverbial other shoe would drop; it was only a matter of time.

The only thing that kept me grounded and gave me a bit of normalcy were my occasional phone conversations with my best friend, Sahara, even though I couldn't let her know what was going on with me. She thought I'd been having guy troubles—which wasn't too far from the truth—but I also didn't let her know that Rafe and I were together. She'd simply chalked things up to my ex being the idiot he'd always been, and I allowed her to believe that.

After Rafe's revelations last weekend, I hadn't known what to do, other than indulge him in what he was willing to give and take from me, giving him the time he needed; the time he thought I needed as well. Not once did I ever imagine he would blame himself for my kidnapping, but it did explain a lot about this whole 'let's not rush into things' mentality he had since my rescue. With that said, we managed to break past certain barriers; working to the degree of intimacy we once shared. Granted, things were progressing slower than I would have liked, but I could honestly say I was happy.

I was taking my morning shower when I felt the most wonderful sensation coming over me. The feel of hands roaming my naked body made me moan. Every inch of my skin felt tantalized by the caresses, then I felt the slight nip at the delicate spot below my ear. Arching my back and closing my eyes, I cherished the feel of the invisible hands that knew exactly what to do to build up this raging ball of fire, which threatened to turn my insides into molten lava. As the shower water began to cool, the clashing difference of my elevated body temperature against the cold water that rained down over my body made me shiver in anticipation of my pending eruption. Imagine my less than delightful surprise when these sensations came to a screeching halt, leaving me with a longing for a blissful release that never came.

Letting out a sexually frustrated growl, I was greeted by a boisterous manly laugh on the other side of the bathroom door.

That's it!

I was going to have my way once and for all with him. I didn't care if I had to tie him up while he slept, beg and plead, heck, maybe I should just get him drunk. Regardless, he was in for it and before the day's end.

Turning the water off and leaving the shower stall, I proceeded to dry myself off, wrapping the towel around my underwear-clad body, and my mind immediately went to work, making sure my link to Rafe remained shut as I devised a plan. I couldn't help the smirk on my face, satisfied with my deviousness as I walked out into the bedroom. Rafe stood there, shirtless and in his boxers, a playful smile reaching his eyes.

You're so in for it.

Turning away from him and facing the closet, I was picking out my day's outfit when I felt his warm body against my back.

"I love," his lips made contact with the top of my shoulder, "that look," he trailed another kiss up to my lower neck, "you get," another kiss toward the sweet soft spot below my ear, "when I get you," this time, he nipped at the same soft spot before turning me to face him, "all hot and bothered." He finished with the pièce de résistance, which was the most sensual kiss I had felt from him in weeks that made my knees buckle and him groan as he caught and lifted me by palming my butt. Gasping, he took the opportunity to plunder and explore the depths and warmth of my mouth. Needless to say, I was there in my underwear, forgetting all about the clothes I was attempting to find.

After a delightful make out session on our mattress—and much to my dismay—Rafe tried to exit the bed, to his own detriment, as I grabbed his arm and pulled him back down.

"Where do you think you're going?" I wrapped my arms around his shoulders and let my fingers play with the hair at the back of his head as his body covered mine once more.

"Breakfast." He kissed me quickly before propping himself up again, as I let my arms slowly trail off of his body, sending visible shivers through him.

I watched as he got dressed in his pajama bottoms, then headed for the door, pausing to take another look at me before he left the room with an, "I'll be right back."

I lay there in nothing but my bra and underwear, smiling at the remnants of the feel of him all over me. Yes, I was frustrated he'd left me without a release, but the hungry look in his eyes told me he wasn't as nearly done with me as he wanted me to think he was.

To be honest, Rafe's sudden playfulness was contagious, so I decided to have me a little fun of my own. Sending him glimpses of things I envisioned myself doing to him—some I was sure should be considered illegal, if not downright dirty—I was met with a growl followed by a tortured, "Payton," from the bottom of the stairwell.

"What?" I said innocently through our connection, with the most obviously exaggerated tone of guiltlessness I could muster.

"You're in so much trouble when I get back up there," he said, a heavy, lustful undertone present in every word.

My entire body quaked with delicious anticipation.

Breakfast had been simple and delicious to say the least; yogurt and fresh fruit mixed with a bit of granola, not to mention a great cup of coffee on the side to chase our orange juices. I hadn't heard any commotion in the house as of yet today, and I couldn't help but wonder what was going on. Where was everyone?

Rafe smirked as he divulged the news. "They're out of town on business for the day."

"I don't think I like this business of kicking everyone out because we want to pleasure each other." I blushed then narrowed my eyes on him. "I should have known there was a reason for that bit while I was in the shower."

He laughed then fed me a strawberry. "Relax, sweetheart." Grabbing on to his wrist, I wrapped my tongue around his fingertips, taking the fruit. "They planned this little trip long before I concocted this plan," he groaned.

"And they've gone where, pray tell?" I said as I chewed.

"Ah," he paused for dramatic effect, "that, my queen, you will find out all in good time. All you need to know is it's just you and me until tomorrow morning."

I scrunched up my nose at the mention of my latest title, getting a chuckle from him in return.

Two could play at that game.

"Well, my king…" I smiled sweetly as his gaze froze to mine; evidently, he hadn't expected for me to address him as such, when he knew full well it was going to be his title someday. "What do you recommend we do now that we've been left to our devices?"

RAFE

Reading her mind, we spent most of the day in bed, watching movies and cuddling. The numerous tender moments thrown in there, with their fairly PG-13 nature, combined with Payton's sexy mind link games, I could feel my resolve beginning to melt. I had an inkling our respective carnal thirsts would be quenched before our heads rested on pillows for the night, if this kept up.

Payton admitted her kitchen skills were slightly limited, but she'd felt the need to treat me, since I'd been waiting on her hand and foot as of late. Since I'd mentioned Italian was one of my favorites—she indulged me with a recipe that had my mouth watering the entire afternoon—or it could have been the fact Payton looked damned good cooking in my parents' kitchen in nothing more than one of my shirts, her hair pilled at the top of her head, looking at ease and relaxed.

My stomach rumbled with hunger as I poured us each a glass of cabernet sauvignon while Payton proceeded to mix the pasta with her homemade sauce, then brought the large dish to the table, along with the basket of cheesy breadsticks she'd whipped up an hour earlier.

With soft music in the background that kept us entertained throughout the last few hours, I took my seat at her side, waiting as she plated my serving for me.

Our meal was spent exchanging coy glances and making small talk. I loved that Payton was finally able to let loose a bit more, her laughter coming out more frequently. Things were feeling somewhat normal again, and for that, I was glad.

By the time Payton collected the dishes, telling me to sit tight while she plated us a simple vanilla ice cream treat for dessert, I had enough of the brewing sexual tension that had surrounded us since my plan to toy with her while she showered this morning.

Quietly making my approach, I positioned myself directly behind her, pulling her body into mine as she poured chocolate syrup over our iced treat. Wrapping my arms around her, I nuzzled the soft spot below her ear, which never failed to make her relax into me and open up to my ministrations.

Turning in my arms so she could face me, her eyes shone playfully while she still held the spoon she was using to serve our dessert, ice cream about to slide off of it and muttered, "What?"

Like a five-year-old sneaking a piece of candy without permission, I leaned in toward her hand and took the melting mouthful before it covered her fingers, then smirked.

Before I knew it, she grabbed onto the sides of my face with a laugh and pulled my mouth down to hers; the taste of Payton and melted vanilla cream an aphrodisiac that set my blood from a slow simmer and cranked it up to full boiling.

The sound of the spoon hitting the floor as she pulled me closer, pressing our fronts together, had me groaning.

It's time.

PAYTON

Rafe pulled away from me, our breaths labored from that delicious kiss. I could tell he was struggling to keep away with this newly acquired knack for withdrawing of his. Don't get me wrong; his desire was present. If I couldn't see it in the tension of his gorgeously structured jaw, the swell of his lips, or even his eyes, I sure as hell felt it down below as his body remained pressed against mine, his cock begging for release.

"Payton," he breathed. "I–"

He didn't get to finish his sentence. I kissed him hard and aggressively, making sure I poured every ounce of my own heated desires into him before I pulled away and pressed my forehead to his.

"I need you right now." I didn't care I sounded as if I was begging; he needed to be clear on my feelings.

To say that was all it took and he bedded me properly, like the man I knew he was, would have been a miracle in it of itself, but such was not the case. To my chagrin, he pulled away flustered, sexually charged—as was I—then gave me his back. His shoulders were hunched forward, his head in his hands, with a loud sigh escaping his lungs.

I tried to fight back the tears that threatened to betray me, and when I couldn't any longer, I turned my back on him and began to straighten up the kitchen—the ice cream all but forgotten—melted, mixing itself in with the choco-late sauce. Moments later, I heard the front door open and shut and the roar of a car's engine revving.

Rafe had left; no last words, nothing.

I finished cleaning the kitchen. I have no idea how I managed it all, what with the constant stream of tears leaking down my face as I worked every soiled surface. I poured my frustrations, my anger, and my sorrow into every part of the chore, even opting at handwashing the dishes instead of using the dishwasher, because I just needed something to occupy my brain.

It was only seven thirty, but this emotional roller coaster had reached the end of its track. I had finally given up, accepting my defeat—my rejection. I headed upstairs and changed into a nightie and crawled into bed after brushing my teeth and washing the day's grime off of my face; resolving perhaps sleeping the rest of this miserable day away would be my ticket.

Maybe tomorrow will be better.

But I doubted that.

I didn't know how long I was out for, but I woke up to soft hands wreaking havoc over my body, sending hot licks of electricity, which only fueled a burning urgency deep within my core. I tried to ignore it, convincing myself it was all a dream, but when I felt my body being rolled onto my back slowly, the scent of my man and his weight carefully distributed over me, I slowly opened my eyes.

It wasn't a dream.

Those beautiful violet orbs that matched mine were staring back at me with urgent need—and remorse.

"I'm so sorry," he whispered, as he brought his face down to my neck and nuzzled my jaw. Then he began to trail tantalizing kisses all over me, alternating between kisses and his sweet apologetic words, repeating the pattern over and over until I felt convinced we were both on the same page for once in the last two weeks.

With a light push, I rolled Rafe onto his back, not once letting my eyes leave his. My hands acted of their own freewill as I straddled his waist, a smile playing at the corner of his lips as he accepted my ministrations. I could feel his arousal pressing urgently into my covered core as I sat myself upright on him, proceeding to slowly pull up on my nightie, teasing him as I revealed inch by inch the skin burning only for his touch. Shimmying down his legs, I kissed his lips, working my way down, caressing his heated skin tenderly as I moved lower on his body. Pulling down his boxers, I alternated between slight nips, licks, and kisses while my hands started to work their tantalizing magic back up, but not before I had weaseled myself out of my lacy briefs.

I fought the urge to speed things up with every pant, breathless moan, and groan that rumbled out of his mouth. I wanted to savor this moment for all it was worth—as if it was our first time again—and repeat this series of events over and over again if I was able to get away with it, because once wouldn't ever be enough.

After our third session, I lay in Rafe's arms, the scent of sweat and passion floating on the air, satisfaction thrumming through every nerve ending, and a sense of peace leaving me feeling invigorated, not to mention, exhausted.

"I wish I hadn't been so damn stubborn." Rafe kissed me lightly on my forehead, while our arms were wrapped around each other. I lifted my head and looked up at him, wondering what he was going on about. "We could have been doing that all day yesterday." I couldn't help the chuckle that came out or the blush that flushed through my entire body.

Bliss was rudely interrupted when the main door to the house slammed shut and a thundering set of feet stomped their way hurriedly to the door to our room, which slammed open against the wall behind it.

There, in our doorway, stood a quite frantic looking Patrick.

CHAPTER 3

RAFE

At first panic hit me. seeing my brother out of breath with worry strewn across his face; then rage flared as I realized Payton was completely naked and plastered to my side.

Pulling the sheet up to cover everything but her head, I snapped.

"Patrick!"

The man's face flared ten shades of red before a smirk played at the corners of his lips, while he averted his eyes from us.

Clearing his throat, in what Payton had observed over the short time she'd been staying with us as a Nottingham nervous tick, he said, "Right…Uh…Why don't you guys get dressed and then we'll talk." Then he quickly exited and closed the door behind him.

"Son of a bitch," I cursed, as I jumped out of bed and proceeded to put my clothes on, Payton following right behind me.

I sure hoped the initial look on my brother's face didn't truly confirm the sense of foreboding that was quickly overwhelming me.

PAYTON

My worst nightmare was coming true. Not the part of being the queen of the Fae realm, but more so the fact I hadn't a clue on how to lead my people. Sure, I had most of the knowledge on how our world works, but I had the theory and none of the practical experience at this point. In all fairness, I felt perhaps my jumping into this role of mine might have been rash—yes, I actually felt some regret with regards to my decision now. As proud as I was to be stepping up to my destiny, and attempting to fulfill my responsibilities, I simply couldn't get past the feeling someone else would have been better suited to assume my role as leader of the Fae world. Even if it were someone of non-royal descent. After all, Will and Sandra knew more about it all than I ever had—good instructors to have—but the problem right now was that after multiple attempts from Patrick to reach his parents, Will and Sandra were nowhere to be found.

I couldn't believe my ears when Patrick explained to Rafe and me, Kristie at his side, he had headed out last night to look into a few leads that seemed suspicious, at Will's request.

So that's what they were all up to? Checking out leads?

A family had been murdered the previous night, and a few random violent crimes, along with a riot that had taken place at my former place of work, Slick's, were only a few events he named having taken place over the course of a few days.

I felt like the world around us was beginning to crumble beneath our feet.

To prove these happenings—not that I didn't trust my match's brother, because I did with my life—Patrick laid down two papers dated with today's date.

Port Hope Chronicle
Sunday, May 19

Woman Found Battered Within an Inch of Her Life

It has been said Port Hope is a renowned place for young families to move to and for retirement living. That is, until the multitude of events of the past week; this has most residents standing on guard, in fear, or simply uprooting their families elsewhere.

This most recent event has left a battered woman—who remains nameless for her own protection—within inches of her life has definitely proven that something is amiss in this once peaceful town of Port Hope.

It is unknown if she will pull through at this time. Authorities have said, in a press conference late yesterday evening, they have yet to find the person/s responsible. In a plea to bring peace back, the authorities have notified everyone to stay in after dark, be vigilant, and to notify them should anything seem out of the ordinary. Captain Winters of the PHPD has advised all residents to refuse entry to their home to any unknown person and that 'trying' to be a hero is not the way to go...

I couldn't read any more...

The Port Herald
Sunday, May 19

*Riots, Break-ins, Battery… Oh My! A Letter
to the Editor*

*One would think Port Hope has fallen into the
pits of hell, what with the events of this past week.
We have been held hostage by an incline in criminal
and delinquent activity.*

*A spokesperson from the PHPD has done
nothing but tell us how to live our lives and nothing
about what they were doing to resolve these issues.
How long will it take before Captain Winters and
his team of valiant officers does something to put
this horror to rest? How many disappearances, in-
cidents of battery, and murders will we have to en-
dure before this once peaceful town and its residents
are able to live in peace again?*

*No one knows who's at play here, and it's safe
to say we aren't the only town suffering through this.
I've witnessed the riot firsthand at Slick's, and I
can't help but ask myself if this is ever going to end.
There's an invisible clash that divides us in this
town, just like the others remotely surrounding Port
Hope, and this divide will either destroy this wonderful community or will make it stronger. I ask
you, citizens of Port Hope: Which one will it be?*

-Anonymous, Port Hope

Upon looking at every page, there were stories, letters
and comments like these scattered throughout both papers. My stomach was churning, my appetite for breakfast
completely deserting me.

"What of Andy?" Rafe asked Patrick, after we had pushed the newspapers out of the way.

"I haven't heard from him since earlier this morning, when I told him to meet back here so we could regroup. He doesn't know I haven't been able to get in touch with Mom and Dad unless he's tried them himself," he explained, grabbing hold of Kristie's hand, as she sat there in complete silence the whole time, clearly distraught about the entire situation.

Getting up and pacing away my stress—well, attempting to do so anyway—I grabbed my cell and began to dial Carly's number.

Rafe looked at me with a puzzled look.

I mouthed my aunt's name to him, getting a nod in understanding. Will and Sandy going missing, and those articles I had read, were enough to freak me into giving my one and only relative a call to make sure she was still safe; especially with the chaos going on in Port Hope.

As I hit connect, but I disconnected the call once the front door slammed open and in walked Andy, fury in his eyes, stomping about like a man on a mission.

"Everything is turning to shit!" he shouted.

"Where were you?" Rafe asked.

"You should have been back an hour ago," Patrick added.

Andy gave him a look of annoyance. "Where are Mom and Dad?"

I couldn't stop pacing my worry away as I let the brothers have their little discussion. If something happened to Will and Sandra, I don't think I could ever forgive myself. I'm hoping, with all of this, they had to remain in the dark for their own safety and that was the reason why no one had heard from them.

"We don't know where they are," Patrick announced.

Andrew stiffened up, his gaze filling with worry.

That's when I picked up to the ever-pungent sense of guilt that began emanating from him.

What's that all about?

I looked at Rafe and he confirmed that he seemed to have read into things exactly as I had, only seconds before.

Andrew, Patrick, and Kristie managed to fill Rafe and me in on the goings-on in the towns that surrounded Port Hope. I knew, with all this chaos, something had to give and soon. It was imperative the humans not know of the Fae world: crucial the balance of things be maintained.

How do I do that though?

People were being murdered, beaten, kidnapped, and I'm sitting here in a mansion, hidden from most of the Fae world, let alone the world in its entirety.

Like a coward.

Something I never was at my core.

A plan needed to be devised quickly and I had no clue where to begin. This is where Will would have been handy. He was always the best at advising.

RAFE

Kristie and Payton were sat silently, while my brothers and I worked on some kind of plan to figure out what we should be doing next. If it were a full-out war, with no need to keep the Fae world from being exposed, then it would have been much simpler—attack. There would be one winner, one loser, and it would be over. Sure, easier said than done in reality, but the humans do it all the time and they were living proof things weren't always cleanly cut-and-dried. Just look at the World Wars or even the most recent events in Afghanistan, Pakistan, and Syria.

When the front door opened then closed softly, our

conversation halted as we turned toward the front of the house.

Carly stood there, a bag in hand. Within seconds, Payton was up, greeting her aunt, holding on to each other until my match's relative stiffened bodily. Wondering what that was about, I turned to the rest of the people who were all sitting with me before her arrival. Every single one of them seemed at ease. All but one—Andy—who stood rigid and frozen to the floor beneath his feet.

"W-what are you doing here?" he asked. I couldn't read the look on his face or in his eyes, but my empathic abilities were telling me he felt a mixture of relief, grief, and pain. Looking over at Payton, I could tell she'd picked up on what I had too.

What the fuck?

PAYTON

Andy was hiding something; I just knew it.

First, there was the guilt he reeked of when we'd discussed Will and Sandy going missing; then, it was the hostility rolling off of him in tsunami waves once Carly had entered the room, not to mention his less-than-desirable greeting.

I made a decision to sit down with him and find out if I could force information out of him. After all, my powers of persuasion could use some practice.

"Hello to you too, Andrew," Carly said sharply, her eyes narrowing on him.

Walking past me, she went straight to Patrick and Rafe, giving them tight hugs, her smile forced but nonetheless present. "And who's this?" She turned toward Kristie, who smiled shyly back at her, as Patrick went to stand behind the newest household member.

Introductions made, we were back to trying to make sense of what could be happening with Will and Sandra. It would have been great to get their take on if this latest plan of ours was going to work or if it was simply a waste of time.

In the Nottinghams' study, Rafe assumed post at his father's desk and had begun to riffle through various books, notes, and his father's laptop to see if he could glean any kind of information that would be to our advantage.

"There's got to be something here to help us out," he whispered to himself, as I entered the room, but no matter where we landed, it was as if we were looking for something that didn't exist.

"Are you okay?" I asked, sneaking my arms around his shoulders for a hug from behind.

He grabbed my hands and brought me down, so I sat on his lap. My man looked overwhelmed and tired, and I wished there was something I could do to make this horrific reality of ours simply disappear and let it be forgotten, but I couldn't.

"I don't know what to do without them," he said as our foreheads touched, looking into my eyes. "What if they don't come back?"

"Then we'll deal with it if the time comes." I held his face in the palms of my hands, trying to appease the feeling of defeat that emanated from him.

The front door came crashing in while we were all congregated in the dining room for dinner, nowhere closer to finding out what had happened to Rafe's parents. Within seconds, I knew something was horribly wrong. I didn't need the smell of blood, the surge of fear and despair to fill the air, and invade my very senses.

Rafe and I looked at one another and were the first to

immediately get up and make a dash for the entrance hallway. What we found broke my heart into pieces, and I didn't know if those shards could ever be put back together for any of us, but especially for the Nottingham boys.

"Andy," Rafe screamed out, "call Lilah, now!"

Who's Lilah?

Rafe rushed to his father's side, ridding him of the dead weight he was holding in his arms. Sandy was bloodied and unconscious. I stood there stupefied and unable to move for the life of me at the horrific sight I beheld. There was so much blood I couldn't tell where it was all coming from; where the injuries were exactly. To be honest, I thought it a miracle that Will was still standing himself. He might have lacked the bloody coating, but he was far from looking healthy. Judging by the cuts, bruises, and welts on him, he should have been on the floor writhing in pain or worse—more like his dear wife—unconscious.

A perfect picture of the walking dead.

CHAPTER 4

PAYTON

I couldn't have been more relieved to find out most of the blood coating Sandra hadn't been her own.

After cleaning her off, Lilah bandaged most of Sandy's wounds, which were mostly superficial and non-life-threatening. It was the hit to her head that had caused her to collapse and remain unconscious.

William, on the other hand, had taken a turn for the worse. Shortly after relieving him from his duty of caring for his wife, he had collapsed into unconsciousness, which manifested itself into the form of a restless sleep. Lilah couldn't do much for him with her witchy powers, but was fairly certain that beyond the scars, William would make a full recovery. It remained to be seen once they both woke up and their conditions could be reassessed.

I still couldn't completely grasp why we hadn't taken them to the hospital. Aside from the places being overrun with the total chaos that was going on, I simply couldn't shake the feeling it might have been a better place for them altogether. My opinion changed slightly once I found out that Lilah did have a degree in family medicine, despite most of everything she had done thus far being witchy in nature.

I stood by and watched as everything unfolded, letting Rafe and his brothers assist in tending to their parents. I knew it was the best thing for everyone at that point in time as Sandra and William lay together, in their marital bed, side by side.

Not necessarily for their sake, but for the sake of their sons, I wished they would wake up; even if it were for a few seconds.

It hadn't taken long for the Fae people closest to them to catch wind of what had happened. As the night wore on, friends and distant relatives had slowly been arriving, congregating—if not overcrowding—the main floor to the home, desperate to lend their support and be the first for updates. So much love surrounded the premises. I couldn't help but feel overly emotional at its presence, the dedication that was shown toward this wonderful couple who'd brought me into their fold; to the royal family and to the throne.

When things grew too intense emotionally, I had to recuse myself to my and Rafe's bedroom for some much-needed time alone. I needed to mull things over and let the family be with each other. Despite the fact we had an overwhelming number of people in the house waiting for news on Will and Sandy's progress, I couldn't bring myself to go down and greet them all. I couldn't bring myself to address their every question and concern as of yet. It had more to do with my lack of faith in myself to lead our people than a lack of information. I found myself wishing I had someone by my side to help guide my path to this unavoidable leadership, but those I trusted most were all congregated in one room

Lying down, hoping I could close my eyes for a few moments, recharge, think, and possibly finally face my duties as a ruler, I didn't expect sleep to find me instead.

I was in some sort of garden, somewhere I had never been. My surroundings were the utmost beautiful sight I have ever beheld.

Footsteps in the distance rang in my ears; the crunching of leaves and twigs, the rushing of wind through the tree branches of the weeping willows that encircled the clearing I found myself in the center of, the sweet scent of the honeysuckle at the forest edging. I couldn't shake the peace and happiness that invaded my senses, or the smile that spread across my face when the footsteps stopped, and I turned to see who had joined me.

"Mom? Dad?"

I ran for them, only for my father—my adopted father that is—to hold up his hand to halt my advances. Coming to a full stop, my smile turned into a frown, and my brows furrowed in confusion.

"But why can't I come to you? I need you now more than ever," I pleaded, but my mother began to shake her head. They both pointed their index fingers in the direction where their gazes were focused, which was directly behind me.

I turned to follow their lead.

A hooded and cloaked woman sat in the dewy grass, a ridiculously cloth and crystal ball atop it, resting in front of her.

What the hell?

She reached out with her wrinkly, taloned hand and motioned for me to come to her with a wave of her finger. The cloaked woman nodded her head, indicating I should sit down across from her. I looked behind, where I'd left my adoptive parents; only to have them both nod in approval and vanish before my very eyes. I couldn't escape the feeling of abandonment they had left me with.

"Before me sits a queen, a symbol of peace and balance," she croaked, reminding me of an ill toad.

This stuff is seriously made for a cheesy movie. It was hard not to roll my eyes at her.

"Child, you are on a path that leads to destruction," she announced.

"How am I supposed to know what to do? I haven't known about all of this for long. Any normal royal would have had a long life of grooming to deal with this war we're facing," I said.

"Hush!" she bellowed. "Pardon, your Majesty." She gave me a slight bow before continuing. "It is not the experience and knowledge in being a royal that matters, but the mere heart and the knowing in what is *right*."

"What's that supposed to mean?" I questioned the old hag.

"I have foretold the rise of two and the demise of the same. The things I've seen nearly a centennial ago still ring true to this day," she said. "When the time is right, child, you shall know what it is that should be done. The loss of loved ones is inevitable and necessary for the outcome which the Fae seek."

"I need to know exactly what to do," I demanded.

All she did was hold her hand up, palm facing me, to halt my progression of words. My frustration was building to a boiling point. I'd seen more than enough palms held up to stop me today, but something about this whole scene before me made me push my frustrations aside and pay attention to whatever message this woman had to give.

"You already know what is needs to be done, child. Trust in yourself, trust in your love for your people, but most of all, trust in your capability of success. Once you've established this trust I speak of, you can only succeed at restoring the true balance." The oracle then bowed her head and folded her hands onto her lap. "You must go, child, your destiny awaits you and war doesn't wait for anyone."

The infamous oracle disappeared shortly thereafter.

Feeling a pull—a voice—I was distracted from the puzzling statements from the oracle. Said voice sounded as if it was getting nearer, sweet and comforting in tone.

I liked it.

I gravitated toward it.

"Payton. It's time, Payton," it called.

I woke to a light rub on my thigh, the contact sending electric shivers of warmth through my body, and with that, I knew Rafe was the one waking me from my slumber.

"Payton. It's time Payton," he repeated.

I opened my eyes to find a beautiful, yet tired, smile on his soft lips. Not knowing how long I had been out for, I bolted upright into a sitting position. Judging by the fact I still felt drained, as well as the fact the alarm clock on my bedside table was reading nearly nine thirty in the evening, I had to have been out for an hour at the most.

"Are you…Are they…?" I couldn't finish. I was so out of sorts.

My worry dissipated the minute Rafe nodded and gave me the brightest smile I had seen since this morning, before Patrick had barged in on us.

I jumped into his arms for a giant celebratory hug.

"They're both awake. Dad's having issues with his speech, and he's not completely coherent, but Mom is able to explain everything. They asked for you immediately, which is why I'm here." He brushed a stray strand of hair from my forehead and tucked it behind my ear.

Kissing him quickly on the cheek, I jumped over him and off the bed then headed for the door. It wasn't until I'd reached his parents' bedroom I paused then turned to wait for a laughing Rafe to catch up and grasp my hand in his before opening their door.

RAFE

I stood at the open doorway, looking at my parents. Despite looking like death warmed over, there was an abundance of life and joy surrounding the two of them. I couldn't help the smile that spread onto my lips, a smile that, upon looking down at Payton who stood by my side, was returned.

Lilah waved us into the room as my brothers, Carly, and Kristie turned to face us, all smiling happily. Their relief was palpable.

Carly then turned toward my mother and leaned into her to kiss her forehead, whispering something only the two of them could hear, despite my oversensitive hearing.

After a few minutes, everyone vacated the bedroom and left the four of us to speak alone—as per my mother's initial request—prior to my fetching my match.

"How are you feeling?" Payton asked, as she settled by my mother's side, the older woman grasping her hand tightly in hers.

Dad had begun to mumble something under his breath that was utterly incomprehensible; off in his own little world.

"Better than him." She turned her head to look at her husband. "William?" She paused until Will turned to her and smiled the most endearing smile I had ever seen my father bestow his wife; the love shared between them very much evident as it warmed the room a few degrees.

"Yes, dear?"

"I think you should have a nap," she told him.

As I stood behind Payton, his gaze locked with mine, then eyes bulged with what I could only read as disbelief and possibly a slight hint of shock.

"No time! No time, Sandy!" He was getting agitated by

the second, and I was pretty sure it was all my fault with the way he was looking at me. I doubted the excitement was any good for him, what with it raising his blood pressure. "Why am I standing behind that lady?" he further questioned. "Wait a minute, there's two of me? Sandra, why are there two of me? Is this a joke? I knew there was such a thing as a doppelganger but—"

If I hadn't known about his head not being right, I would have thought it a joke, what with the belligerent way he was voicing his every thought. His brain behaved almost ADD-ish in nature with the way it bounced around its thoughts.

"No, Will. It's not a joke…and he's not your doppelganger. This is your oldest son, Rafe," she reminded him, holding his hand, worry and annoyance clearly evident in her voice.

"Strapping young man that Rafe of ours, isn't he?" He looked at his wife again with pride. This time, she was unable to contain the slight giggle she painfully winced out. "Hey, Will! Go get my Rafe!" he hollered at me, evidently, still not retaining what Mom had just told him.

In one ear, then out the other.

My mother's suggestion of a nap could definitely do him well.

After a few dozen minutes, and much to my relief, my mother had managed to get Dad to calm down to the point he faded into a deep sleep. I'd also managed to convince Mom to be brought to the spare bedroom, so we could talk without disrupting Dad's slumber.

Lilah agreed. Rest would help make his delirium fade quicker. The sooner he was coherent and of right mind, the better for all of us. Time was of the essence.

PAYTON

Sandra explained everything that happened from their departure the day before to when she woke up in her room, nearly two hours ago. I couldn't believe my ears. The anger that seethed through her, Rafe, and myself could have easily set the entire house aflame should our combined rage been combustible.

Matt and his Fae clan were succeeding in wreaking havoc, but they were progressively getting messier with each hit. Their sloppiness would only lead to exposure, and exposure is what we were trying to avoid.

My mind flitted back to the newspaper articles Patrick had shown us this morning. Something told me it was worse than what these papers were portraying. After all, things happen that don't necessarily make the news or are privy to public knowledge every day.

Rafe explained to me how the Fae factions were spread out across the world where they were able to influence the perceptions of the general human population. They worked solely alongside the humans, but with an aim to keep Fae indiscretions and breaches from being widely known. I had been baffled to say the least, yet not entirely surprised.

"I should have killed the son of a bitch," Rafe growled in fury.

"You couldn't have known this would happen." I patted his lap gently, leaving my hand there to rub soothing circles with my thumb in hopes it would calm him. "If it wasn't him and his minions, it would have been someone else in our opposition."

"Are you kidding me right now?" His eyes pinned daggers my way.

My jaw dropped. I knew he was right to be frustrated,

and to be honest I was just as much, but we'd known chaos would come our way. It was only a matter of time, and it didn't matter who brought it on in the end. It would have to be put to rest.

"Payton's right, Son," Sandra said. "It's not in us to kill for vengeance. You did the honorable thing that day, no matter how miserable it makes you."

"But?"

"But now, we're looking at a different outcome," she proclaimed softly.

"Are you telling me that we're looking at a kill or be killed scenario?" I asked hesitantly, but I already knew her answer.

After what she and Will had been through—and all the other innocents—it was too obvious. Sandy turned to look at me with sadness in her eyes and gave me a subtly confirming nod.

"The longer we wait to act and defend ourselves, the more our numbers will dwindle; the more we risk exposure. And the more people will be harmed, regardless of side or race," she pointed out.

Rafe and I looked at each other, sharing mirroring worried looks. Despite this, the oracles words from my earlier dream came back, and in that moment, I knew what we had to do.

"Thank you, Sandra." I patted her hand and got up to give her a kiss on the cheek. "Please rest. We'll be back in a little while. Rafe, come with me."

"What's the matter?"

"Nothing." And a smirk played at the corners of my lips. I waited for him to exit the room and shut the door behind us before I proceeded. "I think I might have a plan."

Moments later, I was surrounded by everyone who had

come to support the Nottinghams. The house must have had relatively close to seventy people filling the main floor, all of who were waiting for answers now that their concern over William and Sandra had been ebbed. It was time to discuss how we would fight, what are our odds might look like, and what our overall plan and end goal would be, other than survival.

With Rafe holding tightly on to my hand, I gave him a quick glance as the crowd of people followed us to the stairwell off the entranceway to the house. It was easier to make an announcement from there, as I could see everyone from my post on the staircase and vice versa. It was also the largest area that could accommodate everyone.

With one last squeeze to Rafe's hand for support, I began.

CHAPTER 5

PAYTON

I hadn't known of this place—only that it felt familiar—
but I couldn't pinpoint from where exactly. Although it being in a different light, this place seemed like it boded a
romantic feel all at the same time as projecting a haunting
aura.

You're describing the site of a future massacre as romantic?

I snorted at the thought. Something was seriously
wrong with me.

It was the one place where—on this night—where everything would go down.

The one place where some of us would meet our end,
in the hopes that balance could be restored.

And the end to a haunting era.

Standing in the center of the eerie clearing, I awaited
Matt's arrival. He'd agreed to meet on neutral ground at
midnight, and this place was it. I knew I couldn't hold him
to his word; so Rafe and the rest of the Fae who had been
at the house—women and men alike—had come along,
only to remain at a distance, sight unseen, and on standby.
I managed to get my abilities in check enough to create a
partial block with those who accompanied us from the

mansion. I knew it would be difficult to trust and keep a partial block up, seeing as tonight was my first time attempting this feat on a large scale. One that entailed for me to block those on my side, yet keeping my wall partially lowered to read into Matt and those accompanying him.

"How foolish of you," I heard, making me jump out of my thought process.

A shadow emerged from the thicket of trees facing me. Matt had arrived.

There's no turning back now.

"Are you sure about this, babe?" Rafe came into my thoughts with concern.

When we discussed our options earlier, he pleaded with me to wait things out a few more days so we could make our move, but I refused; adamant I couldn't allow anymore death and chaos to take place under my nose. Not without a fight.

With a bit of coaxing, and stating fact after fact that time was of the essence, Rafe came to stand at my side in agreement as we informed those at the Nottingham residence—those who volunteered to come along that is—of how we planned to put an end to the looming darkness.

"I love you and yes," I told him through our link. The only ones who knew about this mind link were Rafe's immediate family. We figured it was better to keep this ability to ourselves, thus giving us a hidden ace up our proverbial sleeves.

"I'm not the one who's foolish here," I pointed out to Matt, who now stood a few dozen feet away from me, a cocky grin splayed across his mouth; one I was too willing to oblige in wiping off his face. With his statement, it more than solidified he hadn't come alone.

Just as quickly as that last thought occurred, shadows began to emerge from the thicket, flanking Matt from all sides.

"Wow, a party just for me? You shouldn't have," I spat. *Coward.*

He was so predictable.

He chuckled. "You didn't expect me to take you at your word that you'd be coming alone, did you? After all, there's no way I'd take the risk, but I see you're not that smart after all. Another reason why royals are completely useless and overrated."

There must have been a hundred men standing all around me. The reality of what was about to happen hit home, and I struggled to stand my ground, worried about those who had come along with us. Hiding my urge to run, I maintained whatever was left of my confident composure.

Don't let him see your fear, I repeated the mantra to myself in an effort to keep my worry at bay.

"We're in trouble," I warned Rafe.

"Is that my cue?" he asked.

Somehow, I didn't know how to answer that question. I trusted I could get away with finding out what the whole deal was going to be, prior to calling my backup into possibly the largest bloodbath in Fae history, but I couldn't.

"What do you want, Matt?" I demanded.

"Funny. I should be asking you that question, considering you're the one who contacted me in the first place. After all, we're all here for you, my queen."

A few of the men standing around laughed at his disdain-filled statement.

"You know what I want," I said, my voice exuding as much power and confidence as it possibly could, seeing as I stood there on my own, trying not to give us away.

"You know that can't be done. But…" Matt tapped gingerly at his chin, an amused light gleaming playfully in his eyes before he continued, "I may be persuaded, if you agree to come with me. I never got to finish playing with you, pet."

"It'll never happen." I tried to sound emotionally detached. "Like I've said before and I'll say it once more. Over my dead body."

"And as I said the first time…" He looked at me, pure unadulterated evil present in his gaze. "…it can be arranged. Everyone knows there isn't a need for a royal and you, my dear, have bought yourself a one-way ticket to extinction."

"In that case…" my voice trailed.

I tried the bargaining angle to see if there was any chance at resolving this in a nonviolent fashion, as much as I knew it wouldn't happen. Matt and his clan were too far gone and out of control with their lust for power and dominance. Noticing movement from the corner of my eye, at the right, I yelled, "Now!" at Rafe, through our link, just as I felt as if a cement wall had come in contact with my body, taking me down to the clearing's floor.

RAFE

Everything happened as quickly as a flash of lightning. First, the rush of bodies through the thicket of the surrounding forest; secondly, as we continued to move into place, I watched as they subdued Payton, taking her into a hold that even Hercules couldn't get himself out of. This plan of ours was far from foolproof in the least, and we knew it, but it was the best we had. My match had stated she'd have herself to blame if we failed, seeing as she had been the one to decide not to wait and put a stop to the mayhem. The sight of my love subdued was all too haunting and reminiscent of the day she had been abducted.

Regardless of her efforts, I still held faith as she kept struggling against her captors' grasps.

"Unhand me now!" she commanded, and much to my shock, their grips began to loosen.

"Don't you dare!" Matt ordered them, and as quickly as those grips gave way, they tightened tenfold.

I felt her physical pain as well as saw it splayed across her face, and my rage had me seeing red.

They brought her to Matt and held her down so she was kneeling, her back to her nemesis. If I could, I would gladly have persuaded her to reach for the knife I had made her hide inside her knee-high boots, but such was not the case. She had mental blocks up everywhere, plus I could tell she was trying not to panic. Trying to reach her through our bond would most likely give us away in this moment.

I was mentally trying to calm myself down, preventing myself from giving in to my urge to fight and attempt rescuing her, knowing my efforts would be utterly useless and unsuccessful, as I'd have to get through our surrounding threats first.

Payton was trapped in a submissive pose to watch the horrors unfold before her as Matt's people made the first move and a large brawl ensued.

Our numbers might have been smaller, but the more I took in our surroundings, whenever I managed to plow through one goon, the more I felt relief that our opponent was dropping in number far more quickly than our men and women.

It looked like we were winning, but my smile had been wiped from my face just as quickly when I got jumped by two much larger, burlier men from either side.

I was coldcocked in the temple.

I was seeing stars.

Then I was helpless.

PAYTON

Shocked at the scene unfolding before me, I wasn't quick enough to warn Rafe.

Tackled to the ground, I struggled to escape the two sets of arms that held me to my spot. Rage seethed through me as I watched the two men pummel my match, my love, my life.

Rafe lay on the ground motionless for what felt like an eternity. He was dragged then dropped at my feet as I was forced up to a standing position above him. His shirt hung off of him, practically ripped to shreds, showing off the bruised, swollen, and bloodied skin beneath it. His face was cut up, an eye swollen completely shut, and his lips were split where blood freely poured from those wounds. I looked for someone to come and help but they were all too busy fending for themselves, their own individual battles.

"Rafe, please wake up," I pleaded via our mind link.

Although he was alive, his breathing was ragged. I whimpered, consumed with my feelings of defeat. I hadn't realized Matt's men had released me until I found myself free-falling down over Rafe's chest, where I buried my face into the crook of his neck. I had to do something, but what? I pleaded to the higher powers that be—yeah, even God—to show me the way.

This isn't the way it's supposed to happen.

"I'll do anything," I whispered. "Please just wake up."

When Rafe groaned, I quickly backed away, my eyes widening in surprise, then I was filled with thankfulness and relief as Rafe started coming to.

Dizzy and with a sudden headache starting at my temples, I knew I only had a short amount of time before the emotional roller coaster of the last twenty-four hours would come crashing down, yet I felt this sort of energy pulsing through me. Something I'd felt before but very subtly; the night I'd been rescued from Matt's clutches. It was as if something had taken over me.

Turning toward my enemy, I found myself moving as though I was a puppet—some kind of external force dictating my every move—it was altogether ethereal with the way I felt, as if I was floating outside of my body. The former Payton sitting back as an observer over my next few actions. One of two things I was aware of was the consuming emotion of sadness and grief for those lives that had been lost this night. Their souls floating away as their bodies remained battered and bloodied on the ground before me. The second reigned supreme over all emotion, however: fury. My eyes burned with a fire that if they could, they would have incinerated everyone in their path of vision. I reached into my boot and felt the cool handle that awaited my grasp.

I sent a prayer of thanks to Rafe for making sure I was armed, even though I'd put up a stink about it.

With my hands down at my sides, in a controlled fashion, I slowly got up, facing Matt and his two minions. Our gazes locked. One of his two goons attempted to push Matt behind them, but I heard myself speak in a voice that barely resembled my own; commanding him to stay in his place.

I will slit your throat here and now before the end of this night, I heard myself think in a voice not my own, despite the fact it had all been in my head.

Sheltered in the recesses of my consciousness, I watched and listened as my body continued of its own accord; always controlled by this invisible puppeteer.

A sense of calm and silence overcame me, my focus remaining intact. The surge of energy rushing through my body, as looks of horror played on every single one of

Matt's people's faces, had me reveling in the power I exuded.

The only one not horrified by these happenings: Matt Davis.

Closing the distance between Matt and me, my feet halted a few feet distancing us. To my surprised delight, his defending duo—the ones who'd held me captive mere moments before—retreated slightly to either of their leader's sides, allowing me full access to the little snake.

This needs to end now! The warrior bellowed inside my head.

I agreed.

"Are you willing to submit?" Matt smirked cockily, but his hesitation, although not audible was palpable.

"Maybe I should ask you the same," I rebutted.

He scowled at my statement.

Hearing light rustling coming from behind me, I was reminded of Rafe and that he'd been coming to when I'd gone all warrior-like.

Slowly, I could feel my puppeteer losing grasp of the strings with this distraction. My normal self was slowly creeping back to the forefront of my mind, as I turned to see what state of consciousness Rafe was in, only to find him being held in a headlock and grunting for air in the process.

Attempting to help my match was futile as an arm wrapped itself around my neck; the other around my waist, pulling me back and choking my lungs of much needed air.

Yes, things did have a quick way to turn around and bite you in the ass when your heart got in the way.

Now, how was I going to get out of this one?

CHAPTER 6

PAYTON

Struggling to get out of the confines of Matt's grip, I felt a cold steel edge sharp enough to carve thin paper-like layers of skin off of my bones, held against my torso. Needless to say, my struggling halted.

A question lingered in my head all this time.

Why couldn't I command him like the others?

Lips that made me want to wretch over the spot where I stood pressed themselves against my cheek, making me shiver in disgust.

"We could have been great you and I," he said against my ear.

My gaze never left Rafe's; his rage evident in his struggling attempt to free himself.

"Let him go," I managed out with what little air Matt allowed me.

He laughed, a cold dry sound of sarcastic amusement. "Now why would I do a thing like that?"

"I'll give you what you want."

The thought that this moment might very well be the end for me surfaced. It became evident to me there would possibly come a time where giving my life to preserve those of others would be mandatory. In this moment, it seemed like we'd all witness the possibility turn into reality.

"No!" Rafe shouted. "Take me." I couldn't help the sad tears betraying me, spilling over my cheeks, sobs completely absent as my body seemed to teeter on the brink of shocked numbness. "You can't do this. They need you."

Matt's booming laughter broke the short silence that ensued Rafe's plea.

"What would I do with you?" Matt snorted, then punched the air in Rafe's direction with his knifed hand, his hold around my throat remaining intact if not growing tighter, causing me to gasp. Now I was really struggling to pull air into my lungs, my eyes feeling as they were bulging slightly from their sockets with the pressure. Stars began creeping into my peripheral vision, and I felt like I was going to black out; that this really was the end for me. As quickly as my eyes began to close, they snapped open with a moment of clarity.

My knife.

Recollecting my right hand held something when my puppeteer had allowed me to come back earlier, after that odd marionette-like possession, I became aware it was the familiar feel of the knife I had slipped out of my boot before. It was wedged in my palm, upside down so the blade was sheathed in the sleeve of my leather jacket. This might be the only time where I would be able to make some kind of attempt at my freedom.

My hope began to rise again, overtaking the despair that had consumed me moments ago.

"I need you to 'fight' for me when it's called for," I calmly told Rafe through our link. When his eyes grew wide to my words, I gave him a forced smirk then winked in reassurance.

"What are you doing?" he asked, but my body was al

ready in motion, ridding myself of the devil once and for all.

I was out for blood, Matt's blood to be exact, and no one else would shed a drop of it tonight but me.

RAFE

I felt the snap in my head the moment Payton chose to block our mind link.

I knew I was posing a distraction—one she couldn't afford in this place and time.

It didn't stop me from pleading with her regardless of that secretive smile, or her saucy wink.

The glistening of the tiny blade in her hand had me seeing a bit clearer.

I breathed easier.

Matt's armed hand was still pointed in my direction as he rambled on, words I was no longer hearing.

I saw the moment my Payton faded away and something more powerful seemed to take over, all within her eyes. As freaky as it was, she seemed to embrace the change and that had me feeling a little more settled.

With a powerful jab, my match sliced through Matt's leg, and judging by the gush of blood, she must have severed his femoral artery.

That's my girl.

Matt's grip around her neck slipped, then she tried to dive away, but not without her nemesis leaving her with a long slice the length of her forearm.

It could have been worse.

Rolling onto her back, I could tell her adrenaline was pumping hard. She kicked up and knocked the blade out of Matt's hand as he attempted to limp toward her, sending it flying out from his reach.

Regaining her footing, she forced a long slice at his outstretched hand, cutting it much like he had her arm.

He toppled to his knees.

The air crackled with the power that consumed her, everyone and everything around us having gone silent.

"You will never have me!" she bellowed, towering over him from behind as she clutched his hair and yanked his head back so his eyes met hers. Bending over him, she sliced at his chest. "You will not be rid of me," she continued. Kneeing him to the back of the head, he toppled over onto his face hard, and I heard the cracking of his nose when his head made contact with the solid earth below him.

The corners of my mouth lifted with a satisfactory grin. My woman was a powerhouse!

In his feeble attempt to crawl away from Payton, she rushed to his side and kicked him in the stomach, which caused him to howl in pain, rolling over onto his back to clutch at his ribs. "You have tortured, murdered, and terrorized so many throughout this pathetic existence of yours. Your time is now up."

Matt was reduced to a quivering bloody mass who writhed in pain, his senses almost deserting him.

"P-please." The fucking weakling.

"Please?" she repeated his word with disgust. "How many times have you heard your victims say that same thing? How many times have you shown them compassion, felt remorse, fought your conscience, and ignored the right thing to do? It's too little too late, Matthew."

Dropping to her knees, Payton straddled his chest. With a swift hard swipe of her knife to his throat, arterial blood spattered up, raining down over the front of her, bathing them in the sweet feel of success I now felt down to my core.

She'd put an end to his miserable dictatorship—his life.

She'd freed herself and us all from the horrors he had brought forth.

PAYTON

The silence that surrounded me after my murderous vengeance was unearthly. It seemed like everything around me had come to a screeching halt. Time stood still.

Now I stood above Matt's lifeless body, taking one last glimpse at him before stepping to the side to face Rafe and the two morons who still had him in their constraints.

"You will let him go or you will face the same end as him," I declared, my weaponed hand pointing down to their former leader's direction for emphasis.

I kept my eyes away from Rafe's; making sure my attention didn't waver away from the situation at hand. I didn't have room or the patience for distractions.

I could feel exhaustion weighing me down, which signaled it all had to end here and now.

Before the two had a chance to react, I caught sight of Andy sneaking up behind Rafe and the duo almost catlike, and knew this would be a bit easier. He carried a rather sizeable tree limb with him. So I waited. With one swift swing, the larger of the two collapsed, tumbling over a kneeling Rafe's right shoulder, his head bleeding profusely, brain matter mixing with the crimson pool. Dead on impact.

Rafe shot out his legs and caught the remaining idiot's feet, knocking him literally ass over teakettle. In that moment, I pounced over him and plunged my knife into his chest, piercing his heart, and watching his eyes glaze over as he fell into the abyss of death.

I felt out of control—relatively wild—and bloodthirsty.

Glancing around us all, I could feel that overwhelming surge of power start to fade and my regular senses coming around.

This moonlit night would haunt us for ages to come, and most likely go down in Fae history as one of the bloodiest massacres of all time.

My heart ached at the bloodshed that had occurred, but also for the souls who had been lost, all for the sake of reinstating balance to our kind. I knew it was a necessity, and that this night was simply the beginning, but it didn't ease my conscience in the slightest.

My body began to shake; a sob caught in my throat and refused to make its way out. Everything remained quiet as people slowly approached, surrounding us, some from our side, some from the other.

My shaking became out of control as my vision began to blur and my knees gave way beneath me. Whatever presence had taken me over was now gone. I was me again.

Crashing to the ground, I clutched my chest at the insurmountable pain and guilt that overwhelmed me. I didn't know what this meant, but what I did know was that darkness was coming for me and there was no more fighting, no more tears, and most importantly, no more fear. There was only peace as I faded out of consciousness, hearing a voice in the back of my mind, lulling me; its words soothing. I would deal with the guilt and pain later.

Warm arms surrounded me. A familiar scent offered me the security I needed. I couldn't bring myself to open my eyes; no matter how hard I tried. No movement. I tried to open my mouth to say something—anything—nothing.

Why can't I wake up?

I tried my mind link and found it completely useless.

What the fuck?

I could hear an exchange of voices in the distance, one

of which lulled me, yet again, into the bottomless pit of darkness.

Clad in nothing but a suit of blood masking the clothes on my back, I found myself kneeling in this all too familiar clearing, nestled in the middle of the dense forest. It was then I remembered it. It was the site of the dream I had about Mom and Dad; the site, which had claimed my innocence and made me a murderous queen.

The scent of honeysuckle, the rustling of the willow branches up above, the dark clouds overhead parting to let the sun shine down over me—as if it shone for me and only me—surrounded me with feelings of peace, soothing me of the thoughts of my transgressions.

Footsteps approached in the distance and I turned to face them. The ancient oracle made an appearance through the thicket.

"You must go back," she said. "It isn't your time."

"I've tried. I can't." My shoulders slumped forward as I looked down at my blood-stained hands, more remnants of the night's massacre.

I couldn't get over the fact I had killed. More than once at that.

To be honest, it wasn't necessarily the fact I had killed per se, more that I had done so with no hesitation and a total lack of emotion. Whatever force had possessed me seemed to have enjoyed the retribution she brought upon her victims too, and that freaked me out. This entity, which had possessed me, was someone I simply didn't care to let take over my body again. She was a maniac.

"Child, there are things in this world that cannot be undone. Brutality, death, despair are all things that need to be dealt with and sometimes are necessary for the greater good," she explained. "There is still much to accomplish."

"We're not done," I said more than questioned, and she

shook her head, indicating the negative. I knew it, but it didn't make me feel any better. I guess it was simply wishful thinking.

"Follow me."

I got up and went with the old hag through an opening in the thicket of trees and dense forest. I could hear water running in the distance up ahead. When she stopped, she held out her hands, taking my offered ones, and silently nodded toward a small body of water, indicating I should proceed forward.

"Tell me what you see," she asked of me, once I had reached the edge of the small stream.

I fought the urge to be my typical smartass self and tell her it was just water running at my feet. She must have known my thoughts, or read into my skepticism, because she wordlessly urged me to look closer.

Focusing on the flowing water, images began to flash by: of Rafe, of the Nottinghams, of a bloody battle I hadn't yet partaken in, the dead we left behind, and more. It was like watching a homemade movie with images of the past, the present, and what appeared like the future. I couldn't help the merriment and the peace that seeped through every fiber of my being.

"Judging by your smile and those tears, I'd say you like what you see," she said.

I wiped at my cheeks and nodded.

"Is this for real?" I motioned toward the stream.

"Have I failed you in the past?" She eyed me carefully and I knew the answer right away.

She hadn't.

Everything she told me had come true. What the Nottinghams and the whole of the Fae world had been told over the ages had been coming true; though some still had yet to happen.

But there was always the prophecy she had foretold: the

royals were extinct. Then again, how could she have seen something, which had been blocked by witchcraft?

Despite that little hiccup, I'd say her point was proven.

"Very well, then. Go," she ordered, then vanished just as quickly as the words rang from her mouth.

I looked around me and felt a pull back to the clearing, my feet assuming the work of their own accord in that direction.

I felt a whisper on the sensitive skin below my ear; gentle to the point it could have easily been mistaken as a caress from the wind that rustled the branches up above.

Rafe.

My match was there to greet me, hand stretched out for my taking.

With a smile, I walked to him, taking hold when the scenery around us slowly faded away to black…

CHAPTER 7

PAYTON

I came to with a vague sensation I was being watched by many. Struggling to open my eyes, daylight assaulted them with my first attempt, so I decided to leave them closed a bit longer, choosing to listen in and make sense out of the presences that surrounded me.

"I think we should leave," a woman said.

My heart skipped a beat as I recognized it belonging to Rafe's mother.

"That means all of you."

I half expected to hear a bit of bickering, but all that came next were huffs and puffs of air as those surrounding me expressed their lack of enthusiasm to leave my side.

Taking notice of the soft surface I lay on, the manly scent that wafted toward me, I knew there was only one presence left in the room with me after the unmistakable click of the door shutting, when the group had exited the room.

The beautiful face stared down at me in greeting as soon as I managed to open my eyes. One glistening eye, while the other was bruised a deep purple and swollen shut; Rafe couldn't have looked any more gorgeous to my eyes.

"Good morning, sunshine," he whispered.

I moved my hand up to cradle his cheek and that's when

I realized my body ached all over something terrible. Every muscle felt like they had gone into spasm. I let out a groan.

"H-hi," I stumbled, my throat parched. Rafe got up from his spot on the bed and rushed to the bathroom, only to come back with a glass of water, which I took eagerly, taking a sip before muttering a croaked, "Thanks." I downed the rest of the water, the liquid gliding down my roughened throat lining, cooling its burn, then handed him the glass as I attempted to sit up, muscles protesting, making me wince in the process.

Rafe rushed to put down the cup and helped me by setting a few pillows behind my back.

"Better?" he asked, and I shook my head, giving him my best mischievous glance. I held my index finger up and wagged it, indicating for him to come closer. When he was close enough, I leaned forward and kissed him softly, pulling away before nuzzling his nose. "Now?"

"Mmm." I closed my eyes, leaning my head back against the headboard smiling. "Much."

His hand brushed my cheek as he eyed me attentively, his face filled with worry. "How are you feeling?"

"Like I have muscles over muscles that haven't been used before, and I abused them. Other than that–" my words were interrupted by my grumbling stomach.

He smirked before saying, "Hungry?" I blushed then nodded. "I'll see what I can get for us."

"Rafe?" He paused and turned around, a look of confusion fused to his face at why I was using our mind link instead of my words. "Just making sure that I'm still me."

His confusion seemed to grow.

"What do you mean?" he asked, taking a few steps back toward the bed and kneeling down to the floor beside me, at which point I took note of my bandaged arm.

"S-something happened to me out there," I said, an eerie shiver creeping up my spine.

"We don't have to talk about it right now." He got up and kissed my forehead sweetly, then pulled away. Meeting my eyes, he gave me that reassuring smile of his. I felt myself calming. "I'll send someone in to keep you company while I'm gone."

Sandra came in shortly after Rafe left the room. As roughed up and frail as she still appeared, she still managed to put off that aura of power and authority she always projected. The woman was amazing.

"How are you feeling?"

She smiled sweetly before leaning over to kiss the top of my head, proceeding to sit down on the chair by my bed. "I feel as though I should be the one asking you that question." I could feel the warmth and kindness in her words.

"I'm sore but I'll survive," I told her. "How's William?"

"He was here earlier. He's relatively back to normal. I guess the sleep helped him, but he's still missing pieces of that night. He's lying down right now, but I doubt I'll be able to keep him away once he wakes up," she said. "We're all so proud of you, Payton."

"For what? I didn't do anything different than what anyone else would have done." My brown knitted together. "What? It's true. Would you have sat back and watched friends, family, acquaintances, what-have-you decimate each other? I don't think so. You would have fought to your last breath, just like I did."

Sandy opened her mouth as if to say something, but all she managed was a nod in agreement.

"Slasher!" Patrick ran in and rushed down to his knees beside the bed, taking my hand as his mother sat there, an appalled—but comical—look on her face because of Patrick's statement and intrusion.

It felt nice to laugh.

"Original, Patrick. Very original." I patted the top of his

hand with my own and noticed some additional movement at the bedroom door.

Andrew stood there, a serious and slightly solemn look on his face. To tell you the truth, he looked as if he were on the verge of tears and only a few words from me would set him off.

"Ah," I tried to lighten the mood as my gaze stuck to Andrew, "and there's BamBam."

I took my hand from Patrick and waved Andy to join me, while I held my hand out for him to take. Patrick moved to stand behind his mother, setting his hands on her shoulders to allow room for his brother.

"Please tell me you'll never go into something by yourself like that again," he whispered.

"It worked, didn't it?" I smirked, but his expression told me he didn't appreciate my cocky demeanor.

"It almost didn't." His eyes held more as they began to tear. "I almost lost two members of my family last night."

"But you didn't." I patted his hand knowing he meant Rafe and me.

Rafe interrupted our conversation, holding a tray with various types of food. I swear he'd brought enough for all of us present.

"Seriously, you didn't have to bring the entire kitchen's contents," I teased, getting a few chuckles from his mother and brothers.

They got up to leave us and my eyes trained themselves on Andy again.

"Andy?"

He turned as he was halfway out the door. "Yeah?"

"Thank you."

He nodded his welcome with a half-smile and shut the bedroom door behind him.

I woke with a start and all alone in the bedroom.

Rafe must have left me after I fell asleep cuddled into him.

Shaking the cobwebs from my mind briefly, I made out what sounded like two voices—one male, one female—in a shouting match.

"If you're going to behave like a fucking three-year-old, you can simply forget it." No one sounded more like my mother—correction, adoptive mother—than Carly. Question was who was she arguing with?

"I'm not letting you get away with it again," the male voice said, followed by some shuffling and the unmistakable sound of a hand slapping against skin. I couldn't pinpoint which man this voice belonged to however.

The doorknob twisted slowly and I decided that feigning sleep might be wise, so Carly wouldn't think I was meddling.

"Fuck off! Don't touch me," Carly spat. "I'm glad I'm leaving tomorrow and don't try to tell me otherwise."

"Fine!"

"Fine."

My bedroom door opened, then shut lightly. On the closing thud, I cracked an eye open and saw Carly leaning her head back on the door, breathing heavily with pain strewn across her face. She looked as if she was fighting tears.

"Are you gonna stand there and cry or are you gonna come over here and tell me what's going on?"

Carly jumped as I eyed her, stiffly sitting myself up. She looked at me, tears running traitorously down her face, and an expression of shock strewn across her features. She hadn't expected to be found with her defenses lowered. With my exhaustion, my emotional walls were all over the place, and so I felt her heart breaking, mine breaking for her. But I could also feel the seething anger boiling deep down inside her, which she was desperately trying to hide from me.

"What's going on, Carly?" I asked.

"It's nothing," she snapped, wiping at her face to erase the remaining traces of her short meltdown.

"I know it's not nothing, Carly, so talk." I folded my arms at my chest. It's not like I had anywhere to go. I could wait all day.

She tried to hold my gaze, battling me with stubbornness. I raised an eyebrow, letting her know I excelled in the fine art of pigheadedness. "So who's not letting you go? I know it's not Rafe, and if you don't tell me, I'll just command it out of you."

Her eyes narrowed to freeze on my gaze. "You wouldn't."

"I would." I paused, watching for a reaction, no matter how subtle, with each name. "Patrick?" Nothing. "William?" I knew it wasn't him. I smirked at her nervousness, smelling her fear. It was all in her face and eyes.

"It's Andy, all right," she blurted out, a pungent smell of frustration and lust overwhelming my senses.

My smirk grew into a full-blown smile and I couldn't help the girly giggle that erupted.

Carly and Andy? Huh! I didn't see that coming.

Well, it sure as hell explained how Carly and Rafe knew each other—seeing as our families never really got together—aside for those few times while we were too young to remember.

Carly spent the next hour explaining to me that she and Andy had a past. It turns out they are matched, but his arrogance, his womanizing ways, not to mention his temper, were all factors that played in their initial relationship's demise.

Carly never fully accepted they're status, and they'd never completed the matching either. It explained why I had never seen her with other guys. One question niggled at me though; how had she managed to stay away from him all of this time, despite his deplorable treatment of her? Rafe had always invaded my mind from the day I laid eyes on him at Slicks, and even more so once we had established physical contact. I empathized with her. It had to have been tough to stay away and rebel against what felt right. I was sure it was even tougher for her right now, since she'd been sharing a house with him, fully aware of their destiny and the far from ignorable pull between two fated individuals.

"We never really ended it officially," she explained.

"I'm confused." I paused, looking at her intently. "You've been dating all this time, haven't you? And I know he's had his fair share of women, according to Will, Sandy, and Rafe."

Carly nodded at all my points, and again I smelled and felt her sorrow and frustration, mixing with jealousy.

"Neither of us had the heart to call it quits, and to be honest, as much as he infuriates me, I can't let him go," she explained. I nodded in understanding at her predicament. "I just don't think he can know that though. He'd rub it in my face if he knew I couldn't let him go."

"And how does he feel?" I asked.

She shrugged her shoulders with a look of despair in her eyes; hopelessness emanating from her, which had me pulling her into my arms for a comforting hug.

"Please don't tell him I told you," she pleaded with me, as she pulled away from our embrace.

"I'll kick his ass for you if he doesn't clue in soon." I gave her a smile, which she quickly returned.

"I might have to let you, what with the fight you put up last night." She was back to her serious, almost motherly demeanor. "Andy told me about what happened. Are you crazy?"

The look on her face, as she scolded me, reminded me of the mother I had grown up knowing. I couldn't help the low chuckle that popped out and quickly regained my serious composure.

"I'm here. I'm with all of you. I'm perfect," I chanted in a singsong fashion, her face losing all of its tension.

"Thank the gods! I thought I'd have to find me a necromancer, bring you back from the dead, and then kill you myself." She chuckled at her statement.

"Listen. I have to talk to you about something," I stated, and try as I might, I simply couldn't get my eyes to make contact with hers just yet.

I wondered if she knew all along, but I didn't think so.

I proceeded to tell her about how I found out that Mom and Dad weren't actually my biological parents. Judging by Carly's reaction, and the slew of frustration, anger, and confusion she emoted toward my questions, she was never aware of this fact. Needless to say, she was never suspicious of anything either, until she found out I was born of royal descent through Andy a few days ago. It was clear; whoever staged the coup had succeeded, flawlessly without a doubt.

CHAPTER 8

PAYTON

Most of the rest of the day had been spent in bed with Rafe at my side. Feeling caged in, especially after smelling Sandra's cooking for nearly two hours, I'd managed to get my match to agree to allowing me to head downstairs and join the clan for dinner.

I was happy everything seemed to be copacetic all around in the Nottingham household so far, but the news about Carly and Andy nagged at me.

Knowing Carly my entire life, then getting to know Andy, I had no doubt they both deserved to be happy. Let's face it; the Fates would have never matched them up if they weren't good prospects for one another. They were just too blinded by their respective stubbornness to work out their differences. If you asked me, they needed a huge shove in the right direction, no matter that Carly obstinately argued with me that no matter what was to change, they'd never work.

"What's going on in that head of yours?" Rafe asked as I came out of the bathroom, refreshed and dressed for dinner. I'd been trying to block him from my thoughts about his brother and Carly, but clearly it hadn't worked. Or maybe the dead giveaway that I was up to something was the shit-eating grin sprawled across my face as I walked toward him.

"Nothing."

"Leave your aunt and my brother alone," he told me softly, as he pulled me into his chest. "You have enough to deal with as it is."

Rafe knew everything. I couldn't hold it from him. Hell, after Carly had left, I was beside myself trying to regain composure on my emotions. So I discussed it with him. It turns out, he had known for a while, seeing as over the years, he'd sort of become Carly's sounding board for all things Andrew.

"But…" I pulled back to look up at him.

He leaned down and hushed me with a quick kiss on the lips.

I groaned and gave him my best pouty face as I pulled away.

"They need help."

"They're grown adults."

Sticking my tongue out to let him know I wasn't at all ecstatic with his cease and desist order, I said, "Fine," then kissed him quickly on the cheek before I turned out of his arms and made my way toward our bedroom door.

RAFE

Everyone was at the table for dinner. After last night's horrendous massacre, it was great to be surrounded by my entire family, even if some of those members seemed to be at odds with others.

Warning Payton off of my brother and Carly's relationship mess was clearly not working. My match was like a dog with a bone, the way she kept her eyes busy between the two.

She wasn't going to let it go, but for the first time, I found myself smiling. As stubborn as those two were, maybe they needed a push. With Carly living with us for the time being, whatever room she and Andrew found themselves in held so much tension you could cut it with a knife. If was making me fidget if I was in close enough proximity, and I could tell Payton was suffering from the same side effect.

For all intents and purposes, my brother might be a pompous, egotistical, temperamental idiot on the surface, but he also had loyalty, heart, and bravery in spades. Those were character traits which shouldn't be overlooked, if easily dismissed. Not from my perspective anyway. As I sat there, silently stuffing my face, a plan began to form in my mind. I would help my woman, if only to keep control on her meddling.

Payton giggled, then covered my thigh with her hand squeezing it, which had me jumping in my seat.

"Are you two all right?" Patrick turned toward us as he wrapped an arm around Kristie's shoulders and she leaned into him.

It seemed like Patrick had fully embraced the fact he had found his match. They looked quite happy and I was thrilled. Kristie had been through so much at the hands of the Davis clan, as we had come to find out, she deserved her happiness.

"We're fine." I looked at Payton with warning in my eyes. "You sure I can't convince you to leave it alone?" I asked through our link. "Maybe we shouldn't–"

"Not a chance." She removed her hand from my leg, then crossed her arms over her chest, before leaning in to peck my cheek. "You're in this with me now, sweetheart." Then she threw in a wink for good measure, which only made me roll my eyes and shake my head at her antics as if I was annoyed.

PAYTON

Refusing to head back to bed after dinner, we found ourselves in the rather expansive family room for a nightcap later in the evening, the whole of us.

Prior to this, I noticed Andy giving chase to Carly and she, the crafty one she was, managed to find an out from being caught alone with him. Judging by what I was seeing, Carly was the saboteur in all of this, at least, in this moment. It was as clear as day Andy needed to make a point and Rafe was in complete agreement with me.

Will and Sandy were the first to leave and head off to bed, and not too long afterward, Patrick pulled Kristie off to his room to finish what he had evidently started between them as they sat there cuddled, him whispering inaudible things as she blushed. I knew I wasn't the only one feeling the combustible heat between those two as they rose and left the room. Rafe seemed rather relieved when the scent of lust dissipated the moment they had departed.

My match rose to get himself a drink from the kitchen, while I sat there eyeing Andrew as he watched Carly get up, sadness surrounding him as she disappeared into the kitchen, behind Rafe.

"Talk to me." I trained my eyes on him.

"What?" He snapped out of the sorrowful daze he had fallen into.

"You. Carly. I know something's up." I gave him a sympathetic smile.

He shrugged. "There's nothing to talk about."

"Bullshit." I eyed him sternly. "I know that's a lie and so do you."

He ran a hand through his already disheveled hair,

carrying the look of a man defeated before attempting the largest battle of his life.

"I don't know what to do anymore. I really fucked it up," he whispered into his hands, leaning forward, elbows to his knees.

"She's your match, Andy," I said. "You two were made for each other. Last I checked you can't run from that."

"She's right, Bro," Rafe said as he came back into the room. I walked to his side. "Just think of how much you're hurting right now. She's hurting more. You need to clear the air between the both of you before she leaves tomorrow."

"That's what I've been trying to do all this time," he whisper-yelled, evidently avoiding being overheard by anyone else in the house.

Andy's fists clenched tightly at his sides as he rose to his feet.

"You need to check that temper of yours at the door," I warned him.

His face flushed and he seemed to relax as he let out a long, drawn-out breath and chased it with a nod.

"I know."

"You'll find her in her room," Rafe told him.

"Thanks."

"Oh, and word to the wise," Rafe began, causing Andy to turn to face us again.

"Yeah?"

"You refused her first. She's right in holding back and refusing you, you know," Rafe pointed out.

"I know. I wish I had done things differently. I need her and only her. I see that now." Andy looked at his feet, the perfect picture of a shamed man.

"Don't tell us that. Tell her," I said.

"Now go fix it," Rafe interjected.

The brothers nodded to one another and Andy left us

with what seemed like a determined bounce in his step. I let myself fall down to the couch and leaned my head back, closing my eyes. The cushions dipped next to me, Rafe's breath fanned down my neck before his lips tenderly met the soft skin there.

"I hope it works itself out," I whispered to him, feeling his smile against my neck. "What?"

"I love the way you decide to take it upon yourself to fix things," he said.

"Well, it beats sitting around watching those you love being miserable," I told him with a simplistic tone, turning my head and opening my eye to look at him.

"I couldn't agree more."

The next morning, I was relieved my aches were relatively gone and merely a memory of the past. Rafe was still sleeping at my side, his eye having lost a lot of its swelling since I'd iced it for him after we turned in for the night.

Like a creeper, I leaned up on my elbow, watching him as he slept. I was in no real rush to start my day—one which I knew would be filled with businesslike dealings— and who really looked forward to that?

My fingers trailed the curvature of Rafe's brows, over his cheekbones, down to his chin. He groaned, his eyes fluttering open to meet mine.

"Good morning, sunshine," I whispered, as he smiled back at my statement.

I love the way he looked at me; I could have been in a room with hundreds of people and with a simple look, it was like everyone else disappeared and he and I were the only ones left.

"Do we really need to go?" I whined, as Rafe pulled me out of our room an hour later.

"My queen, your duties await you." He chuckled at his playful banter.

"Funny," I mumbled.

He stopped mid-step, turned and pulled me into his chest, wrapping his arms tightly around my waist.

"Just think, the sooner we get down there and deal with whatever we need to be dealing with, the sooner we get back up here." He wriggled his eyebrows at me suggestively, causing me to laugh out loud.

"Point taken." I closed my statement with a quick peck to his lips, but before I could get away from him, he pulled me back to him and attacked my lips hungrily with his, leaving me breathless.

"I needed that." He winked then pulled me down the stairs behind him.

We've been at this whole war talk for hours and my mind was spinning from all the information shared, despite my feeling like we hadn't accomplished much of anything.

Sure, we filled in the blanks of what transpired before Sandra and William had been attacked, but I didn't get how that related to the future business at hand.

Sandy left us to make lunch, then was back in a flash with a tray filled with sandwiches and a pitcher of lemonade within fifteen minutes so we could work through lunch.

William had been up to his usual and must have been up at the wee hours of the morning, considering he managed to gather some information on other factions of Matt's clan around the United States and other parts of the world.

Scotland was currently an area that predominantly remained unstable to an alarming degree.

Will informed us, he and the boys were scheduled to fly out later that evening to meet with the leaders in Glasgow.

"But shouldn't I be there?" I asked.

"We can't risk anything right now. We don't know the full extent of the hostility they've been enduring," William replied.

"But—"

"There's no sense in being obstinate, my queen. We serve you, we bow down to you, but we also mean to keep you safe at all cost," he said firmly.

I knew it was useless to argue with the patriarch of this household.

"Don't look so worried, dear." Sandra approached me and rubbed my arm soothingly, but it did nothing to ease the heavy sinking in my stomach. "They'll be back in a few days, and we'll know exactly what we'll be dealing with."

I nodded in understanding.

"Now," Will began, eyeing each of us. "I suggest you get your bags packed and tend to your individual affairs."

I felt so out of control as I watched Rafe pack his bag. Frustration expressed with each item he threw or shoved into his suitcase. He hadn't spoken a word to me since before we left the den, but being an empath has its perks in the sense that I didn't need words to know what his feelings were. I waited until he walked by me, so I could grab on to his hand, then pulled him over so he stood between my legs. He dropped his shaving kit immediately as sad eyes met mine. Dropping down to his knees, I cradled his head into my chest, my fingers playing through his hair.

"I swear if you're not back after two days, I'm coming to find you," I whispered into his tresses, tilting his face up so I could gaze into his violet eyes—eyes that matched mine.

His soft hands began a rubbing pattern on my thighs, warming more than what he touched. He rose to meet my lips and lay us down on the bed, his arms wrapping around me.

I felt safe.

I felt loved.

All because of him.

CHAPTER 9

PAYTON

In case you've managed to formulate assumptions that Rafe and I had done the nasty, you could take those thoughts and shove them up your ass. Instead, we lay there, wrapped tightly around each other, enjoying our proximity, and committing everything about each other to memory. I know, I know, cheesy right? No one truly understands this until they've found themselves in the same exact predicament I found myself in.

Late into the night, Rafe left me with words of love and kisses that lingered all over my face from the front door.

The ladies of the house stood idly by as we watched our men drive away.

I couldn't help the tears as mine and everyone else's worry overwhelmed my empathic senses. Even Carly seemed to be bothered by the men's departure—Andy's more than everyone else's, if I'm being honest.

I wonder what happened last night?

I made a mental note to find out. After all, I could use the distraction.

Two days passed and promises to call and check in were broken by the men. I couldn't help the unsettling feeling that coursed through me as I slipped into bed on this dark, moonless night. I felt like a storm was coming, one of monstrous proportions. I craved—no, scratch that—I needed to hear from someone. To be honest, I gave up on waiting a day and a half ago. Giving into my urge to hear from them, I dialed each and every one of their cell phones to no avail. Again, last night, my attempts at contact had failed and tonight, on my third night without any reassurance, I found myself wide-awake, yet exhausted with worry.

I didn't realize I had managed to fade into a restless sleep until I was rudely awakened by the front door slamming shut and thunderous footsteps rushing up the stairs.

Rushing out of bed, I hid behind the bedroom door, ever at the ready should anyone dare intrude the confines of my room with Rafe's childhood baseball bat—which I'd grabbed from the shelf on my way to my hiding spot—at the ready.

The silhouette who entered was evidently that of a man. He slowly crept toward the bed and paused whence he realized no one was there. That's when I pounced; a beautifully executed roundhouse kick to the side of his knees sending him tumbling to the floor, his head hitting first, knocking him out instantly as I manned the bat, holding it above my head with both hands.

When I realized my intruder posed no threat, I heaved myself to my feet then rushed to the bedside lamp to shed some light on the scene.

I wasn't ready for what I saw.

There on my floor laid Rafe, sprawled out.

Dropping the bat immediately, my hands flew up to my mouth, muffling the surprised, yet shocked squeal that came out. I let myself drop to the floor at his head and cradled it onto my lap, worried that perhaps he'd hit his head too hard. I closed my eyes and cursed myself for not paying closer attention before.

Tears burned to be let free, but I refused to let them come by closing them.

"Not the kind of welcome home I was looking for," Rafe groaned, which made my eyes snap open as he lifted an arm to his temple.

Light footsteps made their way up the stairs, which I presumed those belonging to the rest of the men.

"I'm so sorry," I whispered. "It's just…" my voice trailed.

"I was practically begging for it, barreling in here in the middle of the night." Switching from his sore head to cupping my cheek, he looked up at me with a sweet smile on his face. I helped him to his knees, so he faced me.

"Still," I paused. "I'm so sorry, baby." I peppered light kisses over his face, making him chuckle as he pulled me into him; a hold, a hug that soothed each and every nerve of mine, making me forget of the exhaustion and worry I had been suffering through since they'd left.

Eventually, he got up and pulled me with him, picking me up and laying me down, he rushed to his side of the bed, stripping himself down to his boxers, then crawled in beside me. A large sigh filled with relief and exhaustion escaped him as he pulled me into his chest.

"Sleep. I haven't slept in days," he whispered groggily, and I felt myself lull into a welcoming dark abyss of slumber.

I woke to an empty bed. Sitting up quickly, I wondered if it had all been a dream but to my delight, I saw the clothes Rafe had worn just last night still scattered on the floor.

As much as it had annoyed me in the past, I couldn't help but smile at the mess right then. Yeah, I'm a clean freak, so sue me.

I quickly got up and ran for the bathroom, the urge to go find my man a strong one.

There, I found a note on the mirror.

Good morning, Beautiful,
I didn't want to wake you, but we'll be waiting
for you downstairs. Take your time.
Love,
Rafe

I smiled then jumped in the shower.

RAFE

By the time Payton joined us, Mom was just finishing up with preparing breakfast for everyone.

The room was filled with the aroma of eggs, bacon, French toast, and then some, and after barely eating anything decent for three days, I was chomping at the bit to dig in.

All eyes turned toward my match as she proceeded to find her place by my side at the dining room table. Every man in the room—but me—sported a smirk on their face.

Payton paused after gaining her seat, then peered at me as if silently asking if she'd missed something.

Patrick didn't let her wonder too long.

"So we heard you floored him," he teased, cuing her blush. "Good on you." He winked as Andy and my father chuckled.

The ladies looked confused and that's when I recounted the story, educating them on what happened after I had barged in like a Neanderthal, then tried to sneak into our room last night.

My mother snuck up on me, smacking the back of my

head. "Have you lost your damn mind?"

Payton giggled. "It's okay, Sandra, I don't think he'll be doing that again."

"Well, not in that fashion, anyway." I leaned over and kissed her lightly on the cheek before whispering, "I can think of other ways that would be far less painful and much more enjoyable," so no one else heard.

Payton tried to swallow the bite of toast she'd popped into her mouth, but my words must have put her off-kilter enough that she sputtered then coughed.

"Are you all right, dear?" Mom asked, her as I rubbed her back with a satisfied smile.

Blushing, she nodded and proceeded to shove more food in her mouth as a way to prevent answering any additional inquiries if they came.

PAYTON

Prior to vacating the table, William had asked to speak to both Rafe and me. Without a second thought, the three of us rose and headed for the den. When we reached Will's desk, I caught Rafe and his father exchanging gazes.

"What's going on?" I asked.

"It appears the situation in Scotland is similar to that of ours," William said. "They've asked for an audience with you, refusing to believe you truly are the heir to the throne."

Even after what they'd heard had transpired here; despite having met my match, seeing the violet eyes, the tattoo, they doubted the truth?

I was a little offended to be honest.

Rafe took my hand, as if knowing of my frustration.

Looking his way, his eyes conveyed my same sentiment.

"I see. So what do we do now?"

Did this turn of events mean those who'd been on our side were wavering in loyalty at this point?

"I say we give them what they want," Will said with such a simplistic tone, crossing his arms over his broad chest, indicating he meant business.

"What?" Rafe interjected. "That's absurd!"

I squeezed his hand which still held mine, making his head snap in my direction.

"Let's hear him out," I told my match softly.

I'll be first to admit, walking into an ambush by myself had been a stupid move, but it had been the only way I could things happen at the time. But now, after experiencing it firsthand, I can honestly say I wouldn't put myself in such a situation again. I understood Rafe's reservations, but I also knew if proof was needed in order to make my people feel safe; to put an end to this divide that existed within the Fae realm, then we'd have to do what Will stated: give them what they asked for.

We had the luxury of planning this time around, or I was pretty sure we did. And if there was anything I was certain of, it's that William, or any of the other Nottinghams, would never deliberately put me in harm's way. Honestly, had Rafe's father been coherent on the night we put an end to Matt Davis and his antics, he would have never let it unfold the way it had.

"There's just one more thing," Will added as Rafe and I had started to get up and take our leave. We settled back into our seats. My heart lurched into my throat, anxiety riding me to my core, no thanks to William and his emotions.

Then he proceeded to blow my mind. Okay, so judging by the green tinge to Rafe's skin, I'd say his mind had been blown too.

At my request, I asked William to give us the night before we provided Scotland with their answer.

Leaving the room before anyone said anything else, and unsure if Rafe was on my tail, I stormed up the stairs to my room and slammed the door behind me. Frustration and shock had me shaking like a leaf as I threw myself onto the bed.

Give an inch and they'll take a mile! Can I not live my life in fucking peace and do things at my own pace? I wondered to myself.

"For fuck's sake," I hollered into the pillow.

Rafe hadn't come up yet. I suspected he wanted to let me blow off some steam. The gym seemed really appealing at this point.

Maybe later.

I was grumbling loudly into my pillow when I heard the doorknob to the room click softly.

"Are you all right?" Rafe asked, closing the door behind him.

I lifted my head from my pillow, noticing the amused smirk on my lover's face. He had clearly caught my grumbling, if not my ranting.

I gave him an exasperated look and let out a huffed breath.

"I can't believe they're asking this of me…of us." My disbelief hadn't waned any in the last ten minutes.

"We don't have to, you know." Rafe took a seat on the bed beside me with a hand rubbing soothing patterns on my lower back.

I knew he was right, but I couldn't shake that a large part of me wanted this.

The part I hated about this whole demand was the lack of freedom to do things on our own terms, like everyone else in our world.

CHAPTER 10

PAYTON

Butterflies fluttered in my stomach as I felt the plane take off. Rafe squeezed my hand reassuringly. I'd always hated the takeoff, but it was the landing that made my body shudder. I'd only been on a plane a few times throughout my life, and the discomfort never seemed to ease with each travel experience. I partially blamed it on my empathic abilities. I knew with my own personal discomforts, my walls were lowered, and the anxieties from everyone surrounding me on this jet were feeding into my own.

"Are you sure you want this?" William asked both Rafe and me.

"Surely, if there was a way out of this, you would have found one. It's not like we can fake it," I told Will softly, squeezing Rafe's hand.

"We could, but I don't know if they'd be convinced."

"What do you mean?" Rafe eyed his father. He too wasn't entirely happy that control was stripped from the both of us.

"We could try bluffing," Will explained.

"What do you think would happen if they didn't fall for it?" I asked.

Perhaps the repercussions wouldn't be as negative as I

envisioned.

"I shudder at the thought of what they could do. One thing you need to know is these folks are a little rough around the edges; more than what we're accustomed to in America. Getting caught in a lie wouldn't do any good for restoring faith in the royal bloodline," he explained.

"But what if we said we weren't, but we were on our way to, eventually?" Rafe interjected, throwing me a look of sympathy and a tight-lipped smile.

"I suppose we could try that route," Will started, "but it's not what their demands are, and you're forgetting about tradition."

"We know what they're damn demands are," Rafe growled, making a few heads turn our way. "And fuck tradition, especially with the way things have evolved in this day and age."

"We have another four hours to figure it out," Will said in a freakishly calm state. "It's not what I want for either of you, at least not in this manner, but it's more complex than what we want at this point in time."

"Hold on!" I stopped our conversation.

Somehow, with this recent turn of events, I had forgotten about who I was. How could I have allowed myself to become so submissive? Rafe and William's eyes met mine.

Straightening myself, a sense of confidence and composure floated over me.

"Am I not their queen?"

The men nodded.

Will was the first to speak. "Go on.".

"Then why am I to give in to their demands? Shouldn't my word mean something? Shouldn't they be the ones giving in to my demands?" I wondered aloud and didn't miss a beat. "Rafe and I being there together should be proof enough for them all. Eye color changes, exchange of abilities aside…if they're so hell-bent on living by tradition, why would this next step need to be taken so hurriedly?"

Will sat silently, taking in my ramblings before being honest. "I don't know."

"Who's to say that next, they won't demand that Rafe and I conceive an heir?" I asked, making Rafe's head snap in my direction, his eyes bulging.

I couldn't help the light chuckle and patted his hand reassuringly before giving both men more of my frustration.

"I realize the royals live to serve their people, but come on! This is entrapment and I won't have it."

"Then it's settled?" William asked. "Your mind is made up?"

"I think so," I mumbled. "It's high time people learn that despite being in the dark all this time, I'm still a force to be reckoned with. I might be new to this whole royal business, but I'm not going to be taken advantage of. If this is the way the monarchy has always been, then it's time for a change, or else, why even bother confiding in a leader who isn't able to make up her own mind about something that should be inconsequential in the grand scheme of things?"

"I agree," Rafe stated, lacing his fingers through mine.

We spent the rest of the flight mostly in silence with the exception of some minor lighthearted conversation. As the plane made its final approach, then began its decent, my confidence started wavering.

Could I really be leading us into a wolf's den by standing up for the royal bloodline and myself, or should I give in to these requests? After all, it wasn't entirely that bad of a demand. Something told me I needed to stand my ground, though; with that, the doubts dissolved, and I resolved to stick to my final decision.

Angus MacDougall was a respectable man at first

meeting. A sizeable guy in his own right, there was no doubt he was more than able to maintain order over the Fae people of Glasgow and the surrounding areas, as well as assist with governing the whole of Scotland with a few other major players I would be introduced to eventually. Where MacDougall had me feeling at ease immediately, the thought of meeting 'the others' had me on edge.

"William has notified me, my queen, that you and your match aren't planning to follow through with our people's demands." He eyed my and Rafe's intertwined fingers.

Rafe squeezed my hand reassuringly.

"As your queen, my presence here should be proof enough. To contest my word would be foolish." I wasn't entirely confident in my delivery, but I hoped it didn't show.

You know what they say…if you don't quite have it, fake it until you do.

"I'm not the one who needs proof. I know enough about the royal bloodline to know what to look for."

I nodded in comprehension.

"Then I urge you to convince your people—our people—that it's all real. I know they would never force their children to do what they're trying to get Rafe and I to do," I said firmly.

A movement in the hall caught the corner of my eye.
Huh?
I could have sworn I saw…
Nah.

Shaking my head of what I thought I saw, and concentrating on the conversation at hand, I resolved to try and take a nap before dinner. I had to have been seeing things just now.

MacDougall personally escorted us to our rooms, but not before sharing a little insight on things. It was something I would have thought William and Sandra would have addressed with Rafe and me by now; something told me he knew a thing or two about the royal bloodline that even my match's parents seemed oblivious to.

"I simply don't get how you two haven't completed the full transition," he said as he stood in our room's entryway. "No one can go that long without the final step. It's in your genetics; something that goes on with all matched Fae."

Rafe and I shared a confused glance.

Angus had lost me with his words.

Transition?

Completion?

Were we even talking about the same thing anymore?

As he closed the door, leaving my match and me alone, I made a plan to ask our host what he meant, sooner rather than later, then let myself plop backward onto our bed as I finally took in our surroundings.

The room was truly beautiful, decorated with white and light aquamarine colors as accents. It was a room befitting a queen's stay.

"What does he mean he's surprised we've been taking our time with completing the transition?" I asked, letting my head drop to the side so I could look at Rafe.

He sat down on the edge of the bed. "I don't know."

Something seemed to have been bothering him since the plane ride, but I couldn't quite figure it out.

"Are you okay?" I asked, sitting up, then moving so I wrapped myself around his torso, a leg over his lap, the other behind him with one of my hands sliding under his shirt to soothe him by rubbing his lower back.

"Of course." He lacked his usual convincing charm. "Why wouldn't I be?"

"You seem off. Like something's on your mind." I kissed his shoulder through his shirt before reaching up and turning his head so his eyes met mine. His gaze betrayed him, because in the moment that our eyes met, I knew there was something within him he was fighting with; something he was trying to hide.

"There's a lot on our minds." I understood where he was coming from. "Right now, I think we need to bring Dad back in here and see if he knows what MacDougall was talking about."

RAFE

And the hits just keep on coming.

Dad was useless to shine any light on this whole completion business; we ended up bringing MacDougall in. For my father, he had assumed a traditional wedding. Completing our transition was a wedding, but not the kind you're thinking of. It was more of a commitment ceremony, of sorts. Yep, the one demand that I had grown over the last twenty-four hours to accept, until Payton had put a kibosh on it during our flight across the pond that is, just so happened to be the way to finalize Payton's and my bond.

To humans, it's just a piece of paper that legally binds them. To the Fae, it's sacred in a way the law has no place.

MacDougall struggled to wrap his head around how two matched people were able to avoid this final binding process. Apparently, in the Fae world, it was nearly impossible to fight the force that naturally drove matches to 'seal the deal' per se.

It was a force I hadn't felt as of yet.

At least I didn't think I had. Well, not as strongly as Angus described it.

Now, let me put this together for you so you understand. For royals, this wedding isn't your typical one like I've said before; you know, the one with the white gown, the tuxes, the flowers, and the whole shebang. It's a small ceremony performed by a witch or warlock, finalizing the magical binding between a matched pair.

For ordinary Fae, they've been known to get hitched quite early in their relationships, and seeing as it seems to be a trend in the human world, no one typically questions their actions, especially nowadays. Plainly speaking, the ordinary Fae would be united via regular wedding ceremony.

For royals, however, things are slightly different, thus this commitment ceremony Angus told us about. It explained why my father had initially come to the conclusion that they demanded Payton and I get married.

This particular ceremony wasn't meant to be anything romantic in basis and would typically be performed in private.

It was a crucial part of the puzzle I had yet to fully wrap my head around, which left Payton and I far weaker than we could have imagined.

After seeing my woman in action, I couldn't fathom how much more powerful one person could get. Hell, I'd gained more strength and control over my abilities with every passing day, and I knew it was the same for Payton, exponentially.

MacDougall spoke out of concern. "Without this final process, you are both at risk of being torn apart, and judging by recent events, it's been tried."

By the time MacDougall left, I found myself asking for an audience alone with my father, leaving Payton by herself, undoubtedly pondering a variety of what-ifs.

PAYTON

When Rafe took his leave, I caved into my urge to take that nap I so desperately desired. My brain needed a break.

I must have been out for half an hour before I awoke with the most wonderful physical sensations. As I crept slowly to full wakefulness, I realized something was lacking, despite its familiarity. There was a missing link somehow, and it didn't feel right.

But I knew someone was in my room with me.

The moment my eyes opened, I let out a bloodcurdling scream.

It couldn't be!

No one had seen him in weeks. We expected him to be dead for his lack of results in his servitude to Matt, but here he was. Gage was positioned between my legs in nothing but his boxers.

The thunder of footsteps halted in front of my bedroom door, the doorknob turned with no result.

"Get off now!" I commanded.

Gage's eyes widened in response, his pupils dilated, but the obedience I was expecting never came. Instead, I was greeted with a cocky smirk.

Realizing I was close to being fully naked from the waist down, panic began to take hold.

"Are you going to tell me that we don't belong together?" he asked, the banging on the solid oak bedroom door continuing. I could hear orders for me to open the door being shouted from the other side. "Your body says it all."

"My body says nothing in your favor," I spat, which only caused him to sneer at me.

"Oh, Payton, that's where you're wrong." He gently rubbed my bottom lip with his thumb, trailing the rest of his hand down to the tender skin between my breasts as he hovered above me. I shivered with revulsion.

The succubus in me wanted to take control and suck the life force out of him and be rid of Gage once and for all. Something told me those efforts would no longer yield the results I ached for.

Wood splintered with every hit given to the door to my salvation.

"I have my match. We've completed the process," my voice wavered, and I knew he'd caught me in a lie.

"Oh, but you haven't seen a witch, have you?"

"How would you know?"

"You forget how much I know you." He sounded amused.

"You're forgetting that you're about to wish you were dead." My fiery gaze held his, unwavering. "For someone who seems to know a lot about royals, you're forgetting a few key points." The banging on the door continued. "Let me enlighten you. After all, you'll be taking these secrets to the grave with you very shortly when Rafe gets his hands on you."

"Rafe can't do a thing." So sure of himself. "You're mine."

"Far from it."

"We'll see."

"You'll never have my love, and you don't have my mark, therefore you'll never be my match. Get. Off. Me. Now," I hissed, just as a battered fist splintered through the middle of the door.

Thank the powers that be!

CHAPTER 11

PAYTON

The massive and abused hand snaked its way through the hole in the door and reached for the locking mechanism and retracted itself.

In what felt like an eternity, but realistically must have been a few seconds, Gage was ripped away from me, thrown roughly into the wall opposite of the bed, and Rafe was by my side, his arms wrapped in a protective cocoon around me.

MacDougall was holding a violently squirming Gage against the wall.

"Son, you've made a grave mistake," he growled.

Son?

"Back off, old man." Gage tried to pry Angus' hands off of his arms. "She's mine."

Angus' grip never wavered. This man was frightening, to say the least, when angered, making me thankful he was on my side.

"She might have been at one point but she isn't yours anymore." Angus held Gage's gaze. "You've gone and become what I feared the most. I should have known you were your mother's son the minute you showed up here beaten-up, weathered, and sickly looking."

"Leave my mother out of this!" Gage hollered at him. "My happiest day is when she left you and took me with her."

Son?

I couldn't believe what I heard. I pulled my shirt down to hide my waist, all the while watching this exchange of words, the blankets long ago having been pulled up to cover the rest of me, by Rafe.

"But you're a Wright," I exclaimed, snapped out of my shock, confused at all this new information.

"He took his mother's name when she took him away and moved to America," MacDougall announced over his shoulder, refusing to take his eyes off of his kin.

"So what you're telling me is this disgusting creep, this cheater, this lying scumbag is your son?" I asked with a squeak to my voice that reflected the lack of emotional control in the heat of the moment. I was shaking violently with rage, fear, and a slew of other emotions while Rafe held me together.

"I'm sorry." Angus turned to bow his apology with a hang of his head before returning his focus on Gage. "I regret I have to call him my son. Had I known that you were the woman he always spoke of, I would have kept a closer eye on him. He's deceived us all. Rest assured he will be punished."

"Punished?" I asked.

William came in right then, his jaw dropping as he took in the scene.

"For turning against this household and refusing to re-spect the throne, he will have to suffer our punishment," MacDougall stated, and I couldn't help the note of grief that laced his words.

It sounded so ominous.

William caught Angus' gaze. "They're here."

"Help me with this piece of trash," Angus requested of

Rafe's father. He sounded so emotionally detached right then.

"Dad?" he asked softly of the man who'd just condemned him—his own flesh and blood. "Daddy? Please! You can't do this to me." His voice trailed behind him as Will pulled him into the hall.

"You're no son of mine." Angus looked down to his feet, defeat, grief, and humiliation flooding his emotions once his son was at his back. "Please…take him away." He hung his head low. "Do what you must."

"Surely you don't mean that?" Gage pleaded, William holding him as another man, a much burlier one, came to help with the struggling captive.

"I do. Goodbye, Gage." A forlorn Angus walked farther inside the bedroom and away from his son.

When I managed to pull myself together, I asked Angus if I could speak with him alone. Rafe had been reluctant to let me out of his sight, but I told him he could stand outside the room, and I'd let him know if I felt threatened in any way.

I knew there would be no issues.

MacDougall had proven his weight in trustworthiness.

"What will happen to Gage?" I asked without a moment's hesitation after he shut the door to his office, secluding us from prying eyes and ears.

The man avoided my gaze. "He will be handled." He cleared his throat, as if knowing his answer would far from quench my curiosity, but never volunteered more information.

"What will happen, Angus?" I pried more, using some of my commanding abilities.

His head snapped up to my face and he eyed me curiously.

"Did you just–"

I nodded.

"I commanded you. Or at least I tried," I told him.

He looked concerned for a moment then nodded his head in acceptance of my action. Delight shone in his eyes, which made me wonder what the man thought was so amusing in light of what had just transpired.

He beat me to the punch.

"No royal has been able to do that without being fully bonded."

"They haven't?" Angus shook his head. "Oh."

"My queen, it's true what they've said: you'll be the one to restore the balance. Your abilities supersede those of your ancestors. I expect great things to happen in your reign."

"Uhm…thanks, I think."

"Death," MacDougall answered swiftly. "His punishment for treachery, assaulting the throne, compounded with his overall meddlesome behavior, is death."

Fuck, but how could this man sound so clinical about such a harsh fate?

"But…" I, for one, felt relieved to be rid of him, much like I had of Matt and the others, but another part of me, the one that once loved Gage, felt horrified.

"It's our custom. I don't expect you to understand, seeing as you've lived a fairly unknowledgeable and sheltered life, closer to that of humans; this from William himself. The Fae clearly do it differently and you'll encounter various methods of punishment, as well as various levels of tolerance, wherever you find yourself traveling to. Ours, I'm afraid, has remained intact for centuries and because it works for us, we've stayed with that part of our history," Angus explained. I nodded in understanding. "Ultimately, it is your choice to abide by our customs or invoke your own decision since the crime, after all, was committed against you."

"I see." My mind reeled. "What would you and your people do if it weren't a crime against a royal?" I asked, curious to know if his punishment would have been the same, or if the fact that I was of royal decent offered extenuating and harsher repercussions.

"The same punishment would be carried out," Angus confirmed, lifting his eyes to mine with confidence in his response.

I walked by him, toward the den's large windows, keeping my back to him and crossing my arms at my chest. I didn't know what to say. It troubled me to make decisions such as these, albeit being my first major decision where beliefs and customs were drastically different from my own.

"What if I were to overturn the decision of death? What would everyone think? What would they say?" I thought to myself out loud.

"If I may advise?" I turned to MacDougall and awaited his answer after nodding. "I think it would be in your best interest, in gaining supporters, if we kept with custom and treated this situation the same as we've always treated all others of a similar nature."

"Angus." I approached him slowly with an incredulous look in my eye. "He's your son. No matter how much you reject or renounce him, he'll always be your flesh and blood. Can you honestly say you can handle this burden? Can you live with his death on your conscience?"

"I have seen families go through worse." He was right. I thought of those families who had been decimated thanks to hunger for power and feuding, remembering my very own personal account of the battle that took place weeks ago between me and the Davis clan, my parents' murder…all the others, then Angus continued. "My son would have been honorable, respectful, and most of all, he would have wanted to support having a royal. Instead, he chose the path of self-righteousness, power, and greed. Gage hasn't been a son of mine for a very long time now. I chose to ignore the past and welcomed him back with open arms, but clearly that was a grave mistake."

"Thank you for your honesty." I posed a hand on his upper arm in a kind gesture. "I believe I will leave this in your capable hands. Now, I shall let you tend to your affairs, and I shall speak with you again come morning."

Well past dinnertime now, I left MacDougall's office and found Rafe waiting for me a few feet away from the room's door.

He grabbed my hand and pulled me toward ours, which at this point had been turned down for us, trays of food waiting on the large antique desk that graced the windowed corner of the bedroom.

"I took the liberty to request a quiet dinner," Rafe said.

"Thank you." I cupped his cheek with my hand. "You couldn't have read my mind any better, even though I don't have much of an appetite after that conversation."

"I didn't have to. I know you." He took me in his arms and hugged me to his chest. "The vultures will have you to themselves tomorrow, so I figured I might as well have you to myself tonight." He wriggled his brows, which made me laugh slightly.

"Sounds wonderful," I sighed. "But all I need is your arms and nothing more."

After dinner, Rafe drew us a bath. I had never seen a claw-footed tub this large before. Having his flesh pressed against mine, and his arms wrapped around me, filled me with security and peace, which eased me into a state of contentment I hadn't felt since a few nights ago when Rafe had come home. I wanted these feelings of contentment to last forever, uninterrupted, but I knew that was never going to be the case. The sense of larger things on the horizon was overwhelming, and I knew that Rafe felt it as well. Until we completed our bonding and settled this potent feuding, there wouldn't be a moment's peace.

Tilting my head up, I nuzzled his jawbone while we settled into bed. "We need a witch," I whispered.

"Hmm," he mumbled sleepily.

What did that mean exactly?

Was he in agreement by necessity, or had he wanted this prior to us finding out that our bonding wasn't finalized?

It sounded like a yes, right?

CHAPTER 12

RAFE

I awoke to Payton trying to burrow into my side, her whimpering sounds a dead giveaway she was having a nightmare.

My arms tightened their hold around her, knowing that the simple gesture would give the sense of security she needed in her sleep.

It wasn't until I felt her worry that I knew she wasn't sleeping.

"Stop it," I whispered, causing her to lift her head to look up at me.

"I'm fine."

"Are you sure?" I searched her face for any ounce of doubt. Nothing.

"Are you okay?" she asked.

"I'll do you one better." I winked. "I'll show you."

Rolling her over onto her back, I slowly crawled over Payton, kissing and nipping gently at her collarbone, neck, jaw, and up to her ear.

The moan that came from her had me damn near coming in my boxers.

"You don't know how hot that sound makes me," I whispered against the soft spot below her ear, following my words with a harder nip, to which she granted me with another moan.

Painfully slow, I allowed a hand to glide down the front of Payton's body, a path of goosebumps trailing its decent as I headed toward the top of her underwear.

"Please." She captured my lips with hers, demanding more.

PAYTON

Morning came speedily as I woke to Rafe's hand gently rubbing over my arm. We were still naked from last night's erotic escapade. My body tingled in delight at his touch, craving more of his brand of love when I remembered.

The witch!

It had been agreed upon the night before, we were to meet for breakfast in MacDougall's dining room.

Aside from another woman who sat silently, eyeing me in a speculative manner from her perch across the table, I knew everyone present.

"I'm sorry for my tardiness." Angus sat down after being the last to join us. "And I believe introductions are needed. Payton, meet Elizabeth." The MacDougall clan's witch.

She was quite young. Okay, let's face it, I'm used to seeing, or at least picturing, the stereotypical old hag or the Hollywood version, much like in *Charmed*. Yes, more undeniable proof of my sheltered life away from all things Fae. I couldn't help but wonder why Elizabeth couldn't keep her eyes off of me though. It was rather unsettling.

"Elizabeth?" Rafe paused, reading into my anxiety. Setting his fork down on his plate, he placed his hand on top of mine, which rested on my lap. The witch nodded in acknowledgement, but her gaze remained fused to me.

"May I ask you what it is that has you so infatuated with my match?"

"You haven't touched your food, dear," Angus pointed out.

Elizabeth broke her gaze and looked over to our host, blushing shyly as she realized most of us had already emptied half our plates and hers still sat there undisturbed.

"I-I'm…My apologies." She bowed her head.

After our observation, Elizabeth buried her nose in her plate, pretending to be entirely engrossed with the food presented before her.

I immediately began to relax, but only slightly.

I wonder what that was about.

Was she sizing me up?

Was she trying to figure out if I was the real deal?

Would I encounter this with relatively every new person I met from now on?

Were they all skeptical of me, and who I proclaimed to be, or wondering if the stories they had recently heard were true?

Realistically, they were well within their rights to ask these questions, seeing as I basically came out of nowhere, but I refused to be intimidated by anything or anyone in providing those answers.

You could be reading too much into things, Pay.

It wouldn't have been the first time, and I was sure it probably wasn't going to be the last.

Once breakfast was done, Angus escorted Elizabeth on his arm toward his office, while Rafe and I were instructed to follow.

Tomorrow, we were headed back to America, but tonight, we finalize the bonding process, if Rafe will have it that is.

I still didn't know if his sleepy reply from last night was

in fact a yes.

Tonight, we were meeting the local clans at their request. Angus seemed relieved we decided to let Elizabeth conduct our bonding ceremony, with Rafe appeasing me by confirming that he looked forward to the process.

Separated from Rafe for the remainder of the day, eight hours from now, we would be surrounded by hundreds of strangers—with the exception of the few we knew—as we took our final steps to solidifying our Fae bond. Apprehensive of being away from Rafe, William offered to come and check up on me frequently throughout the day. Angus was looking after Rafe between tending to the evening's preparations while Elizabeth tended to me.

"Here." Elizabeth handed me a small sachet bag.

"What is it?" I asked, peering into it, the sweet pungent smell wafting to my nose.

"A mixture of herbs. You'll bathe in them in a little while," she announced. "But now, we need to cleanse your soul."

After learning I'd have to be asleep in order for this to happen, I was thankful I would get some shut-eye but terrified of being in a room, unconscious, with this person who still had me feeling apprehensive. I wasn't entirely sure I could trust her as of yet, despite Angus' strong recommendation.

Elizabeth left my room to make her special tea, and I requested that William be there for the entire process, to which the woman had agreed reluctantly.

Wearing nothing but this long white satin gown, with loose sleeves that fell delicately over my shoulders, Elizabeth indicated that I lie down on my bed. I eyed William, seeking his reassurance as he sat at the desk. Upon his nod, I followed her instructions.

The witch recited a few incantations, peppering my bed with what looked and smelled like rose petals mixed with a slight hint of lavender. Offering me the teacup, I took and sipped it down quickly, seeing as it was now only slightly tepid in temperature. I felt a certain calmness begin to take over: my body turning to jelly, my limbs urging me to give in, to fall back and let myself go. My eyes growing heavy, I listened to Elizabeth's nonsensical words, almost musical in sound, and soothing me to my very core.

Darkness never fully took me, however, not completely. I remember relatively every word spoken, every smell invading my nose, and every minute detail of the visions that played before me. And when the time came to wake, I couldn't remember another time where I'd felt so refreshed.

Elizabeth's soft voice graced me first. "How do you feel?"

"Refreshed and energized. How is it so?" I asked.

"No one truly realizes how much weight our lives actually produce. Our bodies will carry it around if not released properly because our past follows us spiritually. This cleanse was literally a wiping of the slate, so to speak; for you to start anew," she explained.

I looked over at William who sat there, a warm smile on his face, then turned my attention back to the woman at my side.

"How long do we have?" I asked.

"You've been out for nearly four hours," Elizabeth announced. "For someone who hasn't been around the Fae and its realities for all that long, you sure had some cleansing to do."

"I was out for that long?" I asked, disbelief present in my tone. Elizabeth nodded. "It felt like maybe an hour at the most. I mean, I could hear your chants and smell everything."

"It's part of the entire process. Everyone's experience is slightly different, but the visions and everything play their role as well, no matter how insignificant they may seem," she explained.

"Thanks for being here, Will. I think we'll be fine now." I looked at him.

The man got up, kissed the top of my head like a father would his daughter, and left with a quick wink before he shut the door behind himself.

Bathing in that mixture of herbs felt magical. The fragrances were amazing, my skin felt remarkably smooth and, in the end, looked flawless. Like before, Elizabeth was present with her various chants and incantations. She poured a small vial of liquid in the tub, which made every inch of my submerged skin tingle from my fingertips down to my toes. It smelled much like rosewater, but I doubted that's what it was. Regardless, it made me feel fantastic—like true royalty. Never had I been pampered like this or imagined my life turning out this way. I felt silly for doubting Elizabeth and her character. As quiet as she was, she seemed quite sweet.

"I need you to get out, dry off, wrap yourself in the robe I left on the back of the door, and come out to the room when you're done," she instructed.

"Thank you."

She nodded, turned, and left me alone.

I stood in the bedroom, waiting for Angus to stop by. He was escorting me downstairs to the main hall, which was where the ceremony would take place, followed by an evening under the stars. The expansive room doubled as a ballroom, of sorts. I was beginning to think that being high up in the Fae clans had its benefits. Sure, I'd only seen three households: those being William's, Angus', and Matt's.

Their homes were more than large; they were mansions, opulent. Something definitely befitting royalty.

"You look beautiful, my queen," I heard from my perch by the window, as I watched various people trotting onto the property, dressed to the nines as they headed for the large tents in the gardens.

"Thank you." I bowed my head, a gesture of gratitude. "Why do I have a feeling that normally, a ceremony such as mine is never this formal?"

"Because they aren't. At this point in time, it should be different, wouldn't you agree?"

"Hmm." I did.

"I'm thrilled you and Rafe have chosen to hold your ceremony publicly. I can never pass up throwing a formal party." His warm smile played with the giddiness shining in his eyes. "You two have caused quite a ruckus, and since your visit is such a short one, I think everyone—you and your match included—will respect this union and the return of power to the monarchy in a much more seamless fashion than had they been prevented from being present.

"Can I ask you something?"

"Anything, my queen."

"I know why I'm being called queen, but shouldn't there be a coronation of sorts involved to make it official, or does it simply have to do with finalizing the bonding?" I asked.

"What do you think?"

"I think, my dear Angus," I grabbed a hold of the arm he held out for me, as he gestured toward the door, "that you have something up your sleeve. You're a man of many riddles wrapped into multiple others."

His laugh bellowed out, warm and contagious. "Right you are. Now let's get you down there."

"I still think there's something you're not telling me." Angus MacDougall simply patted the top of my hand, which was rested atop his forearm, letting out a chuckle. Who knew how right I'd be.

CHAPTER 13

PAYTON

Oh, Angus had withheld all right.

I felt like some sort of showpiece as he paraded me down to the main entrance through the historic looking home, until we reached his closed office door.

"One last thing before the evening truly begins." He knocked on the door lightly, moving to my side so I could walk ahead of him, once the door opened. When it did, there stood William with the broadest smile I had ever seen him sport, pride shining in his eyes.

"You look absolutely radiant!" He further opened the door to reveal a small crowd of people, knocking the wind out of me in the process.

What were they all doing here?

Before me stood the entire Nottingham family and their matches. Rafe wasn't in the room, based on the quick inventory I took in of those standing before me, which left me with a sense of longing, but my excitement was too potent to focus on that fact at the moment.

"He'll be here in a few, sweetie," William whispered into my ear, reading my thoughts.

My empathic senses were going into overdrive with

feelings of jubilation and pride. Once over the shock of this surprise, I stepped forward in my whitish pearl floor-length gown. I was shocked when I saw it lying in wait on my bed earlier. It fit me flawlessly with its single strap gathered over one shoulder, leaving the other bare, hugging my upper torso and smoothly following every curve of my waist. Floating down to the floor where the material followed my every movement gracefully, I never felt more polished or deserving of my newly acquired title. Every eye in the room seemed to be awestruck; their adoring smiles filling me with warmth.

"You're glowing." Sandy came forth first, hugging me.

I made my rounds quickly, finishing with Carly. Her, I held on to especially longer.

"What are you guys doing here?" I finally asked, as I backed away to look at all of them. William moved to his wife's side. I couldn't be happier, but I was still slightly confused. "It's not like we're getting married." In truth, it wasn't—yet, it sort of was.

RAFE

People milled about, talking animatedly amongst themselves when I reached Angus' office door.

The snicker of the door shutting behind me had everyone turning to see who entered the room.

My eyes sought out the one person I'd been aching to see all day.

In a flourish of silk following her body's movement, Payton turned toward me and my breath stuck. She always looked beautiful, but tonight, she was radiant, amazing…and all mine.

Clutching my chest, our gazes met and held as time froze momentarily until my feet brought me forward of their own accord.

Smiling, Payton reached her hands out to me, which I didn't hesitate in taking into my own.

"Wow!" I whispered, letting my forehead fall lightly to hers. I wanted to hold her and never let her go.

Payton giggled. "My sentiments exactly." She nuzzled my nose lightly with hers.

Everyone faded away as I simply held her in my arms, swaying us from side to side. I wanted to kiss her, maybe muss her up a bit, but before I could do anything, a light knock before Angus entered brought us back to the reality of what was coming next.

The man's eyes were alight with excitement as he first looked at my match, then me. "Ready?"

Payton nodded, her smile radiant.

"Yeah." I followed her answer, my voice cracking, not from nerves, more from the arousal building within me.

"My succubus is going crazy right now," Payton divulged through our mind link as I escorted us toward the office door. "There's just something about you in a tux."

I groaned and prayed the length of my jacket would hide my physical reaction from prying eyes.

PAYTON

The crowd seemed to part like the Red Sea as we made our way toward a gazebo that was decorated with the tiniest of white lights, much like those that laced the canopy of the humungous party tents. There were tables and chairs set up with linens and candlelit centerpieces.

The sun had set, the moon was rising to great heights in the sky, and stars were beginning to twinkle.

It was all amazing.

Everyone stood around the gazebo once Rafe and I

arrived to the center of it, with Elizabeth awaiting us.

"Join your right hands," she instructed.

We did.

She then proceeded to wrap red, silver, and black ribbons, braided together around our joined hands. Rafe's left hand rested on my left hip, thumb rubbing lightly in a soothing manner, as my right shoulder and back leaned against his chest slightly. Elizabeth began chanting words I didn't understand while my eyes were fused to Rafe's. I felt a surge running through me and noticed when Rafe's eyes went wide, his left hand gripping my waist slightly tighter, as he too could feel it.

People began to whisper quietly amongst each other.

Was something not right? Had I just heard someone say 'glowing'? Nah.

I shook the thought off mentally and gave the ceremony my undivided attention.

After the burning of our respective ribbons, the silver symbolizing myself, the black as him, with the pillared candle that was before us, the ceremony ended.

Rafe and I turned to face the crowd surrounding us, our hands unbound, my left hand gripped into his right.

Elizabeth then took the lone red ribbon and joined our united hands, wrapping them tightly with the piece of silk, singeing the knot so the material melted together with the candle's flame, thus symbolically sealing our bond.

Walking around us, Elizabeth descended from the gazebo to join everyone else. "Blessed be," she said, bowing her head at us as a sign of respect.

Everyone followed suit by repeating her words, as Rafe and I looked onward.

Surrounded with sentiments of elation, we walked down the steps to everyone's level and were immediately encased with eager clan members, who—I was rapidly finding out—were from everywhere across the country but also from many other parts of the world as well.

Stumbling as I was hit by a sudden potent feeling of envy and disdain, I looked up into familiar eyes. Eyes I knew somehow, yet I couldn't place.

Shrugging it off, I allowed Rafe to escort me through the throng of people, greeting as many clan members as we could.

Tonight, I learned another interesting fact from Elizabeth herself when she'd caught me fanning myself while exiting the washroom. Tonight's bonding ceremony had woken the already restless succubus within me, that much I knew, but the witch then informed me a heat to consummate our bond—unlike any other I'd ever experienced—would be present. Apparently, I wasn't the only one who suffered from this discomforting erotic urge. Every time my body came in the slightest skin-to-skin contact with Rafe's over the last few hours, he'd groan—and by the smell of his arousal—I knew the possibility of cutting this evening short was becoming ever so realistic. Now, more than ever, I understood why this bonding ceremony was usually done in a more intimate and private kind of setting.

Our first dance together was also our last, as our physical proximity and contact put us both over the edge.

By the time the music ended, Rafe was rushing me inside the MacDougall mansion, away from the starry skies, and up toward our room, leaving his brothers chuckling.

"Git 'er done!" Andy cheered. I turned in time to observe Sandra slapping him at the back of the head, giving him a warning look as Carly tried to stifle her fit of giggles in his chest. It seemed those two had worked out some of their issues, and for that, I was relieved.

Visions of what was coming next caused my knees to weaken and threaten to buckle by the time we reached the bottom of the staircase. Rafe, clearly in a hurry, turned to me and smirked, then grabbed me like a sack of   potatoes, throwing me over his shoulder like I weighed nothing.

He stormed us through the bedroom door, kicking it shut with his foot as he sat me down on my feet.

Pushing him up against the door, I reached to undo the knot of his tie, rubbing my front against his. His hands wandered down my sides and around my hips, pulling me impossibly closer against him.

"Is this how you felt when we thought we had fully bonded the first time?" he asked breathlessly, his lips swollen from our kisses, pupils dilated, and gaze gone wild, gold flecks swimming around in his violet irises.

"M'hmm" I said, trailing kisses up his jaw and back to his mouth, leaving the tie undone around his neck and proceeding to feel each button of his shirt pop out of their eyelets.

Impatience reared its head so quickly that after two buttons, I quickly pulled back and aggressively ripped his shirt, sending the remaining buttons scattering to the floor and eliciting a guttural groan from Rafe, who took that time to step forward, turn me, and slam me with gentle aggression, my front now against the door.

Kissing down my neck and over to my sleeveless shoulder, I felt the zipper to my dress slide down at a torturously slow pace. Rafe's fingers sent fiery licks over the skin he was revealing—and then it happened.

Call it an anticlimactic happenstance, a stroke of bad luck, or a wardrobe malfunction; the zipper broke and got stuck.

You've got to be kidding me!

As soon as the frustration set in, I felt Rafe grab the undone portion of my dress and with a growl that made my core throb in want for him even more, he ripped the rest of the gown down.

I couldn't keep my moan in, even if I tried, as my bare back collapsed against his bare chest with the sheer force of his pulling on my garment.

Shed of all our clothes, Rafe turned then picked me up as I wrapped my legs around his waist and lowered us to the bed. My skin burned, my body ached in its entirety with need to feel him buried deep inside.

I didn't know how much longer I could take it.

As if reading my mind, Rafe knew just what to do to send us into blissful oblivion.

My body throbbed with the aftermath of our lovemaking the next morning. Still feeling my and Rafe's heat present, I hoped that its thirst wasn't going to be as demanding as it was that first time around, or else it would be one interesting flight back for my match and me.

Last night was magical to say the least. Never had I experienced, or even fathomed, I would experience something like that. Mind-blowing didn't even cut it as a description. In fact, I didn't think there was a word to describe what we experienced, so I would just leave it at that.

With my muscles protesting my every movement, I got out of bed and left Rafe sleeping, as I yearned for the steaming water the showerhead had to offer in order to soothe my aches.

Rafe walked into the bathroom as I was brushing my wet hair, wearing nothing but a towel.

"Why didn't you wake me?" He kissed the side of my neck, licking some of the water off of my shoulder. My breathing hitched, craving to let him take me once more.

"You looked too comfortable." I looked him in the eye through the mirror we were facing. "After last night, you deserved the sleep." He chuckled in the crook of my neck as I turned to face him, pressing my lips to his in a soft peck. "Take your shower, I'll get ready and finish packing."

I got dressed and put away my belongings, picking up my torn gown and including it with my luggage before reaching for Rafe's suit. I was reaching into his pockets to remove anything he left in them before laying it all on the bed, ready for packing when I found it.

As quickly as I latched onto the box, there was a loud knock on the bedroom door, taking me away from my thoughts. Apparently, I wasn't hurrying enough for whoever was at the door because as I crossed half the distance from the bed to the door, another knock came with more urgency.

"I'm coming! I'm coming! Where's the–" my voice trailed as I faced a panicked looking Angus, "fire," I finished.

Panic was strewn across his face. "Gage is gone."

"What do you mean gone?"

CHAPTER 14

PAYTON

Somehow, in the middle of our evening, someone had let themselves into the basement where Gage was being held and freed him.

We found ourselves running through every possible scenario, trying to figure out who would be capable of doing this? We knew we had Fae present who weren't entirely fond of the idea of having a royal in their midst again, even though curiosity dictated their need to see a me in the flesh I suppose. My mind floated to that woman whose eyes seemed a little too familiar. Something bothered me about her and I couldn't quite put my finger on it. Sure, there had been a few others, but she stuck out in my mind above anyone else.

Those eyes.

"Come out with it," Rafe urged, bringing me out of my reverie after we found ourselves in Angus' den.

"I…uh… I was just thinking."

My match studied me. "About?"

"It could just be my imagination, but there was this one woman," I explained. "Her eyes." I let out a loud breath. "They were so familiar, like I've seen them before."

"You've seen one of our guests before? Where?" Angus eyed me curiously; seriousness displayed onto his features, lacing his every syllable.

"It's not her per se, it's her eyes," I said ponderously and then it clicked suddenly. "But it can't be," I exclaimed to myself, trying to make more sense of it all.

How could I have been that stupid?

I had stared into those eyes numerous times—when Gage and I had been an item.

"What is it?" Angus pushed an irritated tone ever so present.

Rafe's hand landed on my lap, its electrical impulses bringing me out of my personal pondering session.

"Huh?" I looked up in a slight daze. "Oh. Uh… Angus, what ever happened to Gage's mother?"

"I never heard from her again after she took off for America," he divulged, disgust evident in his words.

Rafe noticed the slight look of alarm that washed over my face. "What's the matter?"

"I think she was here, but it doesn't make sense. Gage told me she died," I told them, then turned to Angus. "You didn't see her around last night?"

I knew that it was futile to even ask that. There had been so many people here that it was next to impossible to meet and greet everyone.

Angus shook his head, indicating the negative.

"If there's one thing I know now, and wished I knew before I married her, it's that she's quite the conniving bitch," Angus stated bitterly, as if he would have been able to prevent his urges to renounce his match and remain alone all these years.

The Nottinghams left without Rafe and me. Angus assured them we'd be fine and back to them on the next flight out. After making a few calls, he had everyone he could possibly rally on the lookout for Gage, but I had a sneaking suspicion he would be back in the United States. That thought was far from comforting, to be honest. It only meant I could expect to see him again in the future.

Today he was supposed to suffer his fate and that was it. Unfortunately, it wasn't the case anymore. Angus was slowly realizing that Lana, Gage's mother, couldn't have acted alone.

"She might be conniving, but there's the fact she wouldn't have been able to stand around and get rid of the two guys I had on watch duty and free her spawn. Someone else had to have helped her," Angus stated.

Rafe nodded in agreement.

We were given the tour of where they kept their traitors and delinquents. It wasn't an easy place to escape from, that much could be easily said.

"You seem troubled." Rafe's hand reached for mine as we sat on the plane awaiting takeoff.

Angus had commandeered his jet to take us back to America. We were the only ones on it, aside from the pilots and one flight attendant. It was a nice little jet that held a small room with a queen-sized bed and a bathroom at the back. There were seats and a table on one side, and a few larger seats with a TV mounted to the wall by the alcove, leading to the cockpit. Quite luxurious if I may say so.

"Just thinking," I told him, giving him a reassuring smile.

"Care to elaborate?" He rubbed circles with his thumb over the top of my held hand.

I noticed the smile in his voice. My mind flittered to the smell of his arousing heat and the urge that was building within me. In reality, the urge hadn't fully gone away throughout our day's dealings; it had merely been suppressed out of necessity.

My eyes turned to meet his, my sense of control abandoning me. It was hard enough for me to maintain control over my succubus, but now that Rafe had heated tendencies, it was hell to keep from always being all over one another. After all, I could barely control myself, so don't get me started on controlling my match.

Thank the gods this is only temporary.

This sudden surge of carnal lust was due to the surge of powers that finalized their exchange during our bonding ceremony. According to Elizabeth, it only happened when the bond was completed and would dissipate on its own.

"N-no," I stammered as his nose began to nuzzle the soft skin below my ear, making me groan, causing him chuckle into my neck.

Sweat glistened off of our bodies as I tried to regain my wits. My breath ragged, my body exhausted, I had all but forgotten about the realities of our world. Rafe was great at that. My mind slowly coming back, I found myself thinking about what I had found in Rafe's suit as I had tidied and packed earlier this morning.

The drive back to the Nottinghams' was a relatively quiet one in the back seat of the cab we took. I was exhausted and all I wanted was my bed, but tension was in the air.

Rafe seemed withdrawn the closer we got home.

For once, I was glad of the time difference. It meant I had an additional five hours of sleep. Those additional hours faded quickly when we walked through the door and there was Rafe's entire family in the living room.

The conversation halted the minute we walked in, their heads turning to look at us.

"Everything okay?" Sandra asked.

The woman baffled me with how intuitive she was.

"Aside from Gage being loose, wars brewing, and my match hiding something from me, everything's great," Rafe blurted.

My head snapped to him. "What?"

He had the audacity to shrug his shoulders with a sheepish look on his face.

Andy's, "Uh oh" was quickly followed by a slap from most likely Carly, who'd been sitting next to him.

My eyes remained fused to Rafe's. Hostility exuded from him, causing me to jump on the defensive.

Choosing to refrain from making a scene in front of everyone, I bid everyone a good night, then stormed my way upstairs without my match.

I quickly changed, washed up, and got under the covers, keeping my back to the bedroom door. Closing my eyes, I wished for the darkness of slumber to take me away swiftly and hopefully before Rafe made his way upstairs.

Unfortunately, sleep never took me nor did Rafe ever come to bed. It had been a few hours since my storming out on him, and I now found myself regretting it instead of facing the situation head on.

Everything was eerily silent, and I knew everyone must have gone to bed. With no other room in the house to take leave in, Rafe had to have either left the house or decided to sleep on one of the couches. I finally decided to make my way downstairs and see why it was that Rafe hadn't come up as of yet.

I made my way downstairs, not knowing what I was heading into, but aware that we needed to talk.

What waited for me wasn't what I had expected…

CHAPTER 15

PAYTON

Sitting on the edge of the couch, one clenched fist resting on his forehead; the other wrapped around a glass with a deep amber-colored liquid, Rafe seemed to be battling with his own thoughts. The frustration and sadness that surrounded him was thick at best. I walked up to the broken man, grabbed his glass, and moved it to the coffee table across from him, setting it next to the crystal decanter that held the same colored liquor as he jumped at the feel of my touch.

He yawned, his gaze refusing to meet mine still. "Why aren't you in bed?"

"I should be asking you the same question." I watched him as he gave me a sarcastic snort as a rebuttal, in place of speaking.

"What do you want, Payton?" he asked after a lengthy moment of silence.

"I want you to come to bed."

"And I want you to tell me everything that's on your mind." He looked at me pointedly. "But we can't have everything we want now, can we?"

My temper got the better of me.

"You want to know what's wrong?" His eyes widened.

"I'll tell you what's wrong!" And I marched to his suitcase, still sitting at the bottom of the stairwell, and removed my findings from the suit jacket pocket, which hid inside its garment bag. When I turned, I noticed his shocked gaze. "This is what's wrong!" I yelled as I whipped the black velvet box at him. He caught it before it hit him square on the nose.

"B-but…" His voice trailed off.

"Never mind. Rafe, I love you, but–"

It was his turn to stop me.

"Now wait a minute!" He got up to his feet. "This is what's got you in this state?"

I nodded.

He began to laugh as he walked toward me. My feet took me away from him almost instantaneously as I dodged him and took his previous seat. I proceeded to take the glass he drank from earlier, downing the rest of its potent contents, which made me scrunch up my face at its strong taste.

"Oh, you think it's funny, do you?" I eyed him, the whiskey burning my core, fueling my infuriation as Rafe kept on laughing; and I mean, one of those belly-busting laughs.

"It is," he said in between fits. "Here." He tossed me the box and I held it in my fingers, looking at it like it was about to sprout eyes or something. "You never opened it, did you?" I shook my head. "Go ahead." He motioned for me to open it, and my fingers slowly went to lift the top of the box.

Humiliation filled me to the brim as I stared down at the contents of the velvet box. There, twinkling back at me, was a pair of diamond pendant earrings.

"I knew I should have had Elizabeth take them up to you before the ceremony, but I wanted to do it myself." He came to sit beside me, and I let my head fall into my hands as I shook my head.

"I'm sorry," I whispered, feeling foolish for assuming it was anything more to begin with.

"Me too." He took the box from me, snapping its lid shut, then dropped it to the table in front of us, and took my hands in his. "I think we've made asses of ourselves enough for one day." He smirked. "Now," his eyes narrowed, "you mind telling me why you seemed troubled about that?" He nodded his head toward the troublesome package that lay on the coffee table.

I blushed. "Not really."

"So you assume I'm going to propose, you behave troubled, and you're not going to tell me why?" He teased me with his cocky tone, tilting his head to the side as he tried to read my face.

"I didn't assume. Well…" I stumbled with my wording. "I-just-didn't-want-you-to-know-that-I-knew-so-that-it-wouldn't-ruin-anything," I blurted then winced.

He laughed.

"Come on." He pulled on the hand he was still holding as he stood up. "Let's go to bed."

"For what it's worth," I started as he pulled me behind him, "I would have said yes."

All I got in response was a snicker.

A week passed, and we still hadn't managed to get any closer to Gage, other than confirming my preliminary hunches had been right.

The man had been spotted locally but remained elusive.

After a bit of looking into things, it happens that some of Angus' guests had noticed Elizabeth heading to the basement shortly after the ceremony. Needless to say, Angus felt betrayed and was hell-bent on finding out what she was up to, but no matter what he did, shy of torture, Elizabeth simply wasn't talking.

Lana, Gage's mother had been apprehended as well and was currently being brought to the Nottingham residence for questioning. I hoped she wasn't as tough of a nut to crack, but I wasn't holding my breath on that one. In fact, I knew she'd be the opposite.

Pacing the living room, waiting for Patrick and some of William's goons to show, my cell rang, startling me. I didn't recognize the number on the caller ID.

"Hello?"

Payton?" I heard the familiar voice of my dearest best friend.

"Sahara?" My voice cracked.

I could tell she was confused, and if I could be entirely honest with myself, she sounded distressed. "Sahara, are you okay?" I swallowed the lump forming in my throat.

No answer.

"Sahara?"

"Payton? Gage is–"

She was cut off by the discernible sound of a skin-to-skin hit.

"Sahara," I cried out into the phone.

"Hello, darling," Gage drawled out into the receiver.

My heart sank into my stomach, bottoming out and leaving me lightheaded.

If he had Sahara, he could very well have the remnants of my friends—the remnants of my family really—because they were all I had left.

Beyond terrified for my friend's life, a sudden pang of anger was rearing itself as I began to see red.

"Gage, what have you done?"

He tsked. "You might want to ask yourself what I am capable of doing."

Goosebumps crawled over my skin as pictures formed in my head of what possibilities Sahara could face at his mercy.

"You touch one hair... Harm her in any way, and I won't hesitate to wring the life out of you with my bare hands, do you understand me?" I yelled into the phone.

Rafe stood before me, lending me strength through the grip he had on my elbow, which undoubtedly prevented me from collapsing to the floor with worry and panic.

"If you find me that is—which you won't." After a few seconds of silence on both ends, he spoke again. "I'll make you a deal."

"I don't make deals with the devil."

"Release my match and my mother and I'll leave it all be," he stated in a simplistic manner.

That was a blow, but there was no way he'd let everything be. That would be too good to be true and everyone knew it was a bald-faced lie.

"You and I know that can't happen," I answered. "I don't trust you past the smell."

"D'you hear that, Sahara?"

I found myself wishing I were a fly on the wall in that room right now, so I could see what in fact he had done to her. I desperately wanted to know what kind of an advantage he thought he had.

Then a thought hit me.

What if Matt hadn't been the true mastermind?

What if he'd been a diversion—a means to a higher power, a coup—nonetheless, something meant to bring down the monarchy I'd claimed.

Gage snapped me out of my thoughts.

"Did you hear me?"

"You were never able to keep my attention, Gage." I smirked as I said this.

"So what will it be?"

"Meet me where everything unfolded weeks ago," I told him. "It's time you basked in the grimness of your defeat, since you were too much of a coward to be there the first time around."

"Done."

"And Gage?" I paused for dramatic effect, my courage found, and confidence filling me completely. "Don't forget to bring what is mine."

"Likewise."

After a few hours of deliberation; more like a think tank of sorts, Rafe, William and I had come to a conclusion: question Lara, meet with Gage, liberate Sahara, and capture and exact Gage's fateful ending.

We had merely stepped foot out of Will's office when the front door to the house opened with Patrick leading the way. Sandra, the rest of the girls, and Andy came out from the kitchen to meet us, curious of the commotion.

There, in one of William's guys' arms lay Lana, knocked out cold with a thick streak of blood running down the side of her face.

"What happened?" William demanded.

"She didn't want to cooperate and refused to shut up, so they," Patrick explained, pointing with his thumb over his shoulder at the two men standing there, "knocked her out."

"Take her to the basement," Will ordered.

The two men nodded their heads and proceeded.

"Lana," I cooed with a sweet voice, mimicking that of a mother raising her child from slumber. "Lana, time to wake up," I said again, but patting far from lightly on her cheek to bring her back.

Trust me, there was nothing more I wanted to do than to beat this good-for-nothing woman to a pulp right now, if it would give me all the answers I needed.

The woman finally stirred, a look of fury engrained deep in her eyes as her sights locked on me, then Rafe and William who flanked my sides.

"Wakie, wakie, Sleeping Beauty," I singsonged.

That only made her flush crimson with fury.

I did most of the talking. After all, my abilities allowed me to be able to sense and gauge feelings. Along with my keen sense of character judgment, hell, I was a damn lie detector with all these abilities of mine. Taking a few steps back, I faced Rafe who came to stand toe-to-toe with me.

"Are you sure you want to do this?" he asked, cupping my cheek in his hand, studying my face for any hesitation. I nodded slightly. "Okay," he whispered and kissed my forehead before stepping back.

I turned to Lana.

The dark part of me I hadn't felt in weeks was squealing with delight.

CHAPTER 16

PAYTON

I tried everything, but Gage's mother had refused to break. She shared a few choice words with us, hinting there was indeed something far greater than we expected at play. Refusing to back down, and unbeknownst to her, I had my own ammunition against her. If physical aggression wasn't the key to getting her to fold, I hoped an emotional angle would gain us results.

Angus walked in, a battered and bruised Elizabeth in his vices, forcefully towing her along behind him as he moved forward. Upon his failing to break Elizabeth and hearing that Gage and Lana were in the United States, he had immediately jumped on his jet and made his way to us.

Lana's eyes bulged out of their sockets, proverbially speaking of course, when she saw the witch manhandled by her ex-husband.

"Angus." Her voice was low, dry, and fear hung in the air around her.

"Lana." He eyed her, a look of resentment present. "What have you done?"

And from zero to sixty, her fear was replaced by muted emotion and a wicked laugh.

"You were always so clueless and I see that's never

changed, that the only reason I stayed for as long as I did was because I knew you had the power to make it happen," she said. "When will you realize your son was the one who should have been in 'his' place?" She nodded toward Rafe, then mumbled, "Ever the dutiful servant to the crown though. I should have known."

"You're delusional. You know as well as I do that no one can control the Fates."

"Gage was supposed to reign. The witch said so herself," she protested.

"The witch." He paused to look at Elizabeth with disdain and pointed at her. "Her mother chose to play with your desires, upon my request, after I saw you for who you really are. Not once did I think that Belle's offspring would be so deceitful. Frankly, when Belle told me what she told you, my suspicions of how conniving, how corrupt, you really are were confirmed. You preyed on a weak witch and a multitude of others, including our own son to do your bidding, therefore condemning them all and yourself."

"He's my match!" Elizabeth shouted at him. "What else could I have done?"

My head snapped in her direction.

"You could have come to me!" Angus shouted.

After another hour or so of argumentative banter that edged toward being entirely out of control, I took over this entire disaster of an inquisition.

Through my commanding abilities, we discovered Lana had been the leader of the ploy to Gage ascending to the throne by usurping Rafe and me. I was unsure what she stood to gain out of it but, eventually, with my death, Elizabeth and he would have been able to rule accordingly. What Lana neglected to foresee was her minions would fail at their tasks. Blinded with their personal obsessions with power, they all played at each other's ambitions and faltered.

I found myself thinking of famous words by a certain Lord Acton: Power corrupts; absolute power corrupts absolutely. Truer words were never spoken in their case.

More than ever, I knew there was no way in hell I would allow these two to roam free to walk this earth again. Not of their own accord.

Question was: how the hell am I to do this without having harm come to Sahara?

As I had weeks ago, there I stood in the wooded clearing, awaiting potential chaos to ensue. The memories of our interrogation fresh in my mind had me frustrated, but the feel of Rafe's pride filled me with the overwhelming will to see this through to its very end.

"You can do this, love."

Rafe's five words made me straighten my stance, holding my head high as I heard the evident rustling of leaves and cracking of twigs in the distance off to my left.

I turned toward the sound.

Sahara made an appearance first, closely followed by Gage wielding a blade in his free hand.

"Bring them forward," I told Rafe through our link.

The air around us shifted to cold.

"Father." Gage looked at Angus, who held his mother's bound arms behind her back. My ex emanated with nervous energy and fear.

Angus remained silent, refusing to acknowledge his own kin.

"I thought I told you to kill her," Lana spat, regarding Sahara. "You're useless!"

Gage flushed crimson with anger. He clearly didn't appreciate being spoken to in such a demeaning fashion.

The next few minutes were taken hostage by mother and son exchanging words of fault and accusation—thus dragging on this whole exchange of sorts.

"I did everything for you, you ungrateful spawn," she hollered over the howling wind. "You couldn't do anything right. If it weren't for me, Matt would have been rid of you after you first approached him. It's a good thing I knew how his head worked. When I opened for him, he was more than willing to comply." She chuckled at her revelation.

I turned to face her and noticed Angus on the verge of an explosion of monstrous proportions. He was shaking with rage and I couldn't blame him. If I were to know my match was with someone else after being matched, I think I would put in every effort to rip him limb from limb, despite the separation. After all, it wasn't for lack of love for his match that led to their demise. Well, not on his part anyway.

The more time I spent in her presence, the more I knew Lana was never capable of loving anyone but herself and her lust for dominance.

"Enough!" I bellowed. "This is how it's going to be."

RAFE

Angus and I escorted Elizabeth and Lana toward Gage as he released Sahara, who ran straight for Payton.

Just as Elizabeth made it to her match's arms, his mother huffing a retort to their ridiculous display of affection, the rustling through the thicket of trees and bushes signaled my father's men working in perfect synchrony to surround the three of them.

With nowhere to go, Gage looked toward Payton in a panic.

This had me grinning in satisfaction.

That's right, motherfucker.

"Gage. Lana. Elizabeth," Darwin, the leader of my

father's defense began. "You have been tried. You have been measured. And you have been found wanting. What say you?"

Payton approached, settling at my side, an arm wrapped around my waist, while still holding on to Sahara with her other, as we watched the scene unfold before us.

None of the three responded.

Silence looming, they were shackled and carted back to where our vehicles were lined up at the side of the nearby gravel side road.

"Are you all right?" I asked Sahara, once the threat had disappeared.

Backing away so she could inspect her friend from head to toe, Sahara shook all over.

"What's going on?" she asked.

"Come on," I tell Payton, grabbing her hand then reaching for Sahara's. "We can talk on our way."

PAYTON

I chose to remain silent, telling myself there would be enough time to tell Sahara all about what's transpired in my life when we got back to the mansion.

It gave me a bit of time to scramble my brain with ways to break the news about the Fae world to my best friend. To my knowledge, humans don't normally know about our world unless they are involved with someone from it. I decided to take some time and confer with William, Angus, and Rafe first, to see where their thoughts on the matter stood. Sandra was looking after a slumbering Sahara who had fallen asleep—probably due to shock—on the car ride home.

Assuring both William and Angus that our secret was safe with Sahara, I confirmed I wouldn't tell her everything about our world, just enough to appease her suspicions of what was going on and to quench her urge to question. After all, there were humans out there that were with Faekind and have been educated on our world. If humans were to be kept in the dark all this time explicitly, it would have been forbidden for Fae and humans to mate.

As Rafe and I walked into the living room, Sahara sat awake, sipping on a glass of water.

The moment her eyes landed on us, her gaze widened. "Mr. Bright Eyes?" Good, she was her normal self again.

Rafe burst out laughing as he came to snuggle me from behind.

"You two?" She took her index finger, pointing in our direction and waved it back and forth, gesturing to both of us intermittently.

"Yeah." I smiled.

"It explains a lot." She took another large gulp of her water before putting the glass down on the coffee table, then getting to her feet. "What it doesn't explain, however, is how you've forgotten to pick up a phone to let your best friend—no, scratch that…your *worried* best friend—know what was going on."

Crossing her arms at her chest, she tapped her foot, hinting that she expected an answer.

"I like her," Rafe whispered against my ear before kissing it.

"Well? I'm waiting," she exploded.

Sahara wasn't really mad, but she definitely knew how to make one feel bad. Clearly it wasn't working on Rafe, seeing as he was now full-out laughing, his face pressed into the side of my neck to muffle the sound.

"I had to leave, and I couldn't let anyone know," I told her.

"Why?"

"Sit down. We'll be a while," I said.

Sahara digested things like I thought she would—well. I told her the bare minimum about our kind. I told her about how Gage, Elizabeth, and Lana had orchestrated a coup to take me and Rafe out.

"What's up with your eyes?"

"This is where it gets weird," I warned.

She looked at me quizzically but patiently waited for me to elaborate on my statement.

My dearest best friend sat there after absorbing all the information my match and I were willing to provide, communicating through our link on what we'd agree and disagree to divulge.

By the time we were done, her mouth was opening and closing as if she was a fish out of water. If all of this had happened without the chaos that had occurred in Port Hope, she might have thought differently of the whole situation. There's no doubt in my mind she would have flown off the handle with our revelations.

CHAPTER 17

PAYTON

SIX MONTHS LATER

These past six months have flown by quicker than I could have ever anticipated. Choosing to embrace my reign as queen fully and completely, with the help of William and Angus, things were looking up for the Fae realm.

Peace wasn't fully restored yet—and may never fully be—but it was evident that things were looking up and well on their way.

It wasn't until our battle in Scotland when things began to really make a dramatic turn for the better. It was also my second battle, and if it weren't for William and our local faction of followers who'd come along, I doubt we would have made it through unscathed.

Refusing to stay behind and be treated like a porcelain doll, I was flanked by Rafe, William, Angus, and the rest of the Nottingham and MacDougall clans on the frontlines.

People were everywhere, cries of torture had rung out, blood plastered my face, as I stood erect from my latest victim to take in the scene before me. It was an absolute bloodbath.

In my immediate vicinity, I spotted Rafe, Andy, and

Patrick surrounded by three other goons who played for the other team. Moments later, I watched as they seemed to have developed their own technique, which took them only a short while to bring their attackers down. Rafe turned in time to see the horror flash in his eyes.

"Payton!" he yelled.

Instinctively, I turned to look but was too late. Darkness enveloped me as I felt my body crumble to the ground with a thud.

I came to, my head cradled on Rafe's lap; plagued with a splitting headache. It turns out I had been taken down by some big oaf with the butt of a club he was holding. One look beside me told me that he had to have died a most painful death. Andy and Patrick knelt at my feet while Rafe was at my side.

"Do you know how close I came to losing you?" Oh goodie, he was irritated.

"Ugh…"

"No!" Everything around us was quiet. "No more. I don't care if I have to keep you under lock and key. I won't allow you into this kind of violence again."

His eyes held mine with promise and everything around us melted away.

The moment I chose to sit up, I winced, which had my match jumping to the task to help me situate myself.

"I think you might be right." I looked up at him as he towered above me on his knees, while I sat leaning sideways into his chest, trying to keep the pressure off of the lump on the back of my head. "On one condition."

"I don't think you're in the best shape to be bargaining." Andy touched my leg. His eyes conveyed how close I'd come to losing my grip on this world yet again.

"I agree." Patrick eyed me.

"Care to renege that condition of yours?" Rafe's eyes

captured mine once he tilted my head up to look at him.

"I'll cease and desist if you promise to lock yourself up with me." I winked and gave him a sly smile. "I can't rule without my king by my side."

The boys began to chuckle.

"I think she's fine despite that goose egg on her pretty head," Patrick stated.

"Woman, you'll be the death of him," Andy chimed in.

Rafe got up with me in a bridal hold and smirked. "Who said I was against that? I think it's a great idea, and I intend to practice our seclusion techniques when we get back."

"Is that so?"

He winked, making me laugh.

"Take me home, boys."

Setting my head down on Rafe's shoulder, I nuzzled the crook of his neck while letting him assume all control.

It was over.

Well, I hoped it was.

The one final thing: my coronation.

Here I was standing in my bedroom, staring down at the lovely light yellow gown I was to slip into. Tonight, was a special night: a celebration as I officially ascended to the throne.

Angus had been thrilled when we told him we had chosen to continue being open with the public with regards to our royal duties; so much so he had been the first to declare himself as the planner for the ball that was going taking place after I swore my oath to our people.

Everyone looked fantastic, dressed to the nines, their masquerade masks strapped to their faces.

Angus had really outdone himself this time.

Gentlemen bowed to their ladies, making the night feel like we were all caught up in some kind of fairy tale.

"I might be forced to end the night right now," I heard in my head, before I felt the electrical contact of his body against the back of mine, sending waves of pleasuring warmth through to every one of my nerve endings.

"You managed to find me in this sea of people." Turning to face him, I gave Rafe a million-watt smile. "You're good."

"Nah, I knew the girls helped you get ready," he confessed. "I asked Carly what you were wearing." He toyed with his bowtie, pretending to loosen it. "You certainly know how to bring a man to his knees." The smell of his arousal was prominent in the air surrounding us.

Seconds trickled quickly as Rafe began to move away slightly, holding my hands at arm's length.

"You're gorgeous, you know that?" He smiled warmly, making my heart melt. "And I love your earrings by the way."

Blushing, I reached for my left ear, touching the cluster of diamonds as I remembered our misunderstanding from months ago.

"It only seemed right to wear them for such a momentous occasion."

"Momentous, I agree." I couldn't shake the feeling there was something more he wasn't telling me. "Payton." He paused and cupped my cheek in his hand quickly, before he took a hold of my abandoned hand again, twisting both of my hands so he grasped them completely in his. "You are by far the most remarkable, strong, brave, and amazing woman I have ever had the pleasure of meeting in my entire life; with the exception of my mother, of course." Everyone around us began to laugh, which made me smile. It was so easy to forget we were surrounded when he got like this. "I feel honored to be fated as your match." My stomach began to churn nervously. "I would like to spend the rest of our days, if you'll let me, proving to you there is no better match out there; that when we are together, nothing can tear us apart." He lowered himself onto the classic singular bended knee. "I know you would have said yes six months ago, had it been a ring instead of those blasted earrings, but as all customs dictate, will you do me the honor, my love, my match, my queen, in becoming my wife?"

I didn't wait.

I didn't answer right away either. Well, not in the traditional way the typical woman would.

Instead, I threw myself down into his arms laughing hysterically as the tears spilled over. I could care less about my makeup. After all, that's what waterproof mascara's for, right?

"Beautiful," I repeated while peppering his face with a series of soft erratic kisses.

He chuckled. "I believe you still owe me an answer."

"Oh, but you knew I'd say yes." I pulled away to look into his eyes, my hands cradling his face. "My answer is still the same, Rafe Nottingham, and it will always remain as such. Yes!"

"What was that?" Andy yelled out within the crowd, which most thankfully had a sense of humor and laughed while a few others gave scolding looks in Rafe's brother's direction.

I loved Andy's sometimes inappropriate humor, and I hoped to the powers that be he'd never lose that part of himself.

Rafe pulled me up so we stood on our feet, faces merely inches apart.

"I believe that was a yes. Is that right, m' lady?" Rafe backed away slightly and gave me a dramatic bow, which I thought was fitting to the theme of the evening and our environment.

I nodded, and everyone erupted in cheers of jubilation as Rafe wrapped an arm around my lower back, pulling me into him for a kiss that would have singed my socks off, had I been wearing any.

Moments later, after he put his ring on my finger, the kisses, the hugs, and the multiple well-wishes, the ascension ceremony had begun.

The crowd parted, revealing a red velvety carpet that I walked down with Rafe as my escort. It was all too over the top, but leave it to Angus and his gifted little helpers to make something so big and extravagant out of relatively nothing.

William had brought in a high priestess, which I later found out was simply a more elegant term for a top-of-the-line witch to oversee the ceremony.

Clad in a ruby red satin robe, she proceeded to expel a dagger from its sheath, which hung from her robe's waistband. I knew of this particular part of the ceremony beforehand, which is why I remained cool, calm, and collected at this point. Not much could be said of Rafe, the Nottingham clan, as well as the guards who Will had brought in for the occasion; they all stood stiff and ready to pounce if one move was made threatening my life.

Cutting the palm of my hand ever so slightly, I felt the sting before the blooming line formed. She held my hand up above the white-pillared candle before us and fisted my hand.

"If you'll please repeat after me."

I nodded.

In some foreign tongue, I did my best to get each word perfect, which believe it or not, it wasn't all that difficult. It was as if, deep inside me, this ancient language and the knowledge to speak it had always been there, lying dormant.

The priestess squeezed my wounded fist over the flame as blood trickled into the candle, turning the flame blue instead of its habitually normal color.

"Benedictus," she proclaimed and I knew, from my various readings that it was Latin for 'blessed be.'

My hand now bound in a white cloth, I was instructed to take a knee and avert my eyes.

I heard the heavy oak doors to the ballroom open and shut with a resounding clang and footsteps making their way toward me, as hushed whispers followed the ooh's and ah's. Moments later, those footsteps halted, and I saw the priestess' red robe before me at my knees.

She put a tiara on my head, which surprised me, seeing as I never expected something like that. Yes, despite the fact I'm known as a queen in the Fae world, I never anticipated being clad in similar fashions as the royals of the human world.

"Rise and behold your loyal subjects," the priestess proclaimed.

I kept my head bowed until my body was fully erect, and that's when I saw Rafe. Nothing but pride and love shined in his eyes. I held my hand out to him and he moved forth and claimed it in his larger one.

Turning to Angus, William, and Sandy, I bowed my head to them with all the appreciation and strong esteem I held for them. If it weren't for their support and unwavering loyalty, I don't know if royal blood would have ever remained in existence.

Staring into his violet eyes, the only eyes that matched mine, we danced and held each other tightly, savoring the evening's outcome. Contentment would be the best description I could use for what I felt at this very juncture in time.

"May I cut in?" I heard behind me and Rafe froze mid-step.

I turned to see the guest who stood before us, the hairs on the back of my neck rising before I took in his features.

A single thing came to my mind as I took in this middle-aged man: violet eyes.

It couldn't be?

As if in a trance, I took his outstretched hand and noticed the middle-aged woman, who claimed Rafe's in hers as the music took us into a waltz.

"You didn't think your mother and I would have missed this, did you?" he asked in a deeply soothing tone.

I turned to my right and eyed the woman dancing with my fiancé and like this strange yet familiar man; she had those same violet eyes.

Only royals have those eyes, Payton.

My eyes widened with shock as I struggled to keep up with my dance partner's steps. Offering a small courteous nod and a warm smile, the woman confirmed my suspicions—no matter how preposterous.

My parents—my biological parents—were alive.

With every beginning, there is an end.

I'm sure my story doesn't end here. In fact, I know it doesn't.

There are many things about this world that cannot be explained. Some are dark, some are haunting, and others are wonderful, perhaps even seen as a gift. I tended to fall in one of those categories. Which one, at this point, I was still not quite sure of, although I did have a slightly clearer picture painted before me. One thing I'd come to terms with was that perhaps I would never completely know, and that was a thought that I was wholeheartedly comfortable with.

Who ever said you needed all the answers in this cruel, deceitful, yet precious, forgiving, and mysterious world?

THE END

ABOUT THE AUTHOR

Born and raised in small town Northern Ontario, Canada, Carey Decevito has always had a penchant for reading and writing.

More than a decade later, with weeks of sleepless nights, she finally gave in and put pen to paper (more like fingers to keyboard!) She submitted to the dreams that plagued her. And the rest, as they say, is history!

A member of the RWA, Carey enjoys spending time with family and friends, the outdoors, travelling, and playing tourist in Canada's National Capital region. When life gets crazy, this contemporary erotic romance author seeks respite through her writing and reading. If all else fails, she knows there's never a dull moment with her two daughters, her goofy husband, and cat and dog who she swears are out to get her.

She is the author of both *The Broken Men Chronicles*, *Nightshade* and *Essence Extracted* series.

CONNECT ONLINE

Website – www.careydecevito.com
Email – carey.decevito@gmail.com
Facebook – http://www.facebook.com/carey.writes

ALSO BY
CAREY DECEVITO

The Broken Men Chronicles series

Once Written, Twice Shy
Almost Forgotten
Play Me to Infinity
To Forgive & Hold Safe
A Heart's War

Nightshade series
Night Break
Night Shift

Essence Extracted Trilogy
Essence Derived
Essence Surfaced
Essence Redeemed

once written twice shy

THE BROKEN MEN CHRONICLES

book one

carey decevito

PROLOGUE

I stared at the overly large bags that lay by the front entrance with what must have been the world's largest *what the fuck* look on my face.

"I can't do this anymore," she said.

Her words tore me to shreds.

"What do you mean you *can't do this anymore*? Julie, you haven't been doing anything to fix *this*."

"I'm done, Paxton."

I ran my hands through my hair, pulling at the handful of blond tresses gripped between my rigid fingers. The prickle in my scalp did enough to keep my temper in check and diffuse some of my anger. "You've got to be kidding me."

I couldn't believe it, but then again, part of me could.

She was giving up on everything.

My love, our life, our family; it had all disappeared in the blink of an eye.

I still loved her, but in all honesty, I can also state that I haven't been in love with her for quite some time.

We've been together for nearly five years. In that time, we had built a home; one that was graced with our beautiful three-year-old son, Jasper.

My hand ran down my face.

Christ, how am I going to explain this to Jasper?

I was willing to try and work things out. Hell, I'd even mentioned marriage counseling on multiple occasions, but like everything else, work came first and the sessions she'd promised had never materialized.

I looked up at the woman who stood in the entrance to what I had considered our home; frustration, anger, bitterness, and that subtle feeling of failure were all too overwhelming. "Fine," I said. "But what about Jasper?"

"Can you keep him for this week? It's just until I get situated. We can discuss custody later."

"Where are you going?"

"Todd asked me to move in with him," she said as if I'd known about her relationship with the man the entire time. I'd suspected she'd maintained her infidelity but I didn't know for sure until now.

I huffed. "So he's still in the picture." I hadn't asked, so much as accused her. She nodded. "How long have you two been–" I couldn't finish the sentence.

Bile rose from my stomach.

"Does it matter?"

"You can go," I said in a defeated tone. I looked down at my feet when all I wanted to do is ask her what happened to *can we try and work things out?* I groaned at the memory and shook it out of my head in dismay. "Get out."

"Pax–" She made to step toward me with an outstretched hand.

I shook my head to stop her, my blood pressure rising with her lack of departure. "I said *get out*!" I pointed toward the door, my stomach contents churning further.

The woman took off like a bat out of hell.

And that was it.

I was tired of having a one-sided relationship and was thus relieved at the woman's departure.

The news of her continued adultery had shocked me, especially when she had sworn to make an effort to sort things out between us. It explained why we had remained in our separate rooms all of this time, living our lives apart as though we were roommates. It more than proved that we were better off without each other. This was really the end of my marriage.

When I married, I had intended it to be for life.

Well, I guess life had a plan of its own, huh?

With each passing day, I picked up the broken pieces of me. I hadn't realized that I had stifled so much of myself over the years to try and please a woman that seemed to never be sated with anything I said or did.

Fueled by my feelings of loss and neglect, I made a decision, which led me to rediscover an old love.

The proverbial flame was rekindled and I began to write again.

For what felt like an eternity, I wrote. When I was done, I read my piece over so many times that my words no longer made sense, forcing me to put it down and go back to it later.

I stared at my finished manuscript displayed on my screen.

What am I going to do with this?

I had discovered a site, a few months before. It had been recommended by a colleague. The venue allowed people from around the world to peruse and read various works written by amateurs. Some of the work on there I found horrid, while others, despite their various grammatical and punctual flaws, you wished you could set your hands on an edited and printed copy, they were so great.

What the hell?

I decided to chance it.

With a bit of copy and paste, and a little restructuring, I hit the *publish* button and there it was. My first written piece was out for the world to see.

It wasn't until a few months after I had posted my work that I stumbled upon a comment that I couldn't dismiss. I ached for constructive feedback, but the lack of it was getting to me due to the site being overrun by teenagers. I debated getting rid of my profile altogether up until that fateful day.

That short message was where things began to change for me. With simple words of appreciation, intellectual and heartfelt thoughts, followed by a click of her mouse, Alissa had made me smile.

I sought her profile out and found that she was a fellow amateur writer just like me.

She's gorgeous, had been my first impression. Despite her evident beauty, something else could be seen in her profile photo; something that beckoned me further, begged my curiosity to look beyond the surface. It was in her eyes.

Loneliness.

Or was I reading into things too much, since I was such a novice at these social media-like sites?

For a few weeks, I sat on Alissa's words alone as I read through some of her work.

She was good.

Better than good even.

I thought that I'd end up with one of those written numbers that didn't make much sense or that glittered in the night featuring vampires and werewolves. Boy was I wrong!

The woman sure knew how to paint a vivid picture. She pulled off the hot and sexy but kept it real all at once by adding emotion, drama, even a bit of action and suspense to her mix. Her work was altogether something reminiscent of everyday life: the good, the bad, the ugly, the... Well, you get the picture.

A few days after reading her last novel, a dream influenced

by her work prompted me to finally write out an acknowledgment to her comment.

From there, we began to chat through private messages on a near daily basis.

We never stopped…

CHAPTER 1

Just short of a year later...

Waiting in the airport terminal, I couldn't remember the last time I had felt like this. The anxiety that consumed me was reminiscent of my first date with my first girlfriend as a teenager.

I looked up at the screen and saw that US Airways flight 2583 to Jacksonville, North Carolina had landed. In a matter of minutes, Alissa would be standing before me in the flesh. My thoughts flittered to that first day, nearly a year ago, when we first made contact.

The conveyer belt that carried the luggage snapped me out of my reverie when it ceased moving and the area around me had become deserted.

Had something gone wrong, had she stood me up?

I lowered myself to the bench behind me and let my head drop into my hands. I sighed. "Serves you right for thinking she'd show," I mumbled.

I was trying to convince myself that I should leave when I felt a soft hand on my shoulder. "Paxton?" a soft-spoken woman said at my side, her voice familiar from our numerous phone calls and Skype conversations.

She's here.

My heart thumped out of my chest. I felt foolish for thinking the worse and excited that I was proven wrong. I got up to face Alissa, who had a beaming smile splayed on her face. Boy was that smile contagious! My lips tugged upward instantly.

She let out a giggle and after dropping her bag, she jumped me with a hug. Without hesitation, my arms found their way around her waist to return her enthusiastic greeting.

"You looked like a man deep in thought."

I set her back but held on to the sides of her arms. "Can I be honest?"

I breathed easier when she nodded, "I wouldn't expect anything less from you."

I shrugged my shoulders sheepishly and averted my gaze from her momentarily before eying her. "I thought you weren't coming."

She looked as if I'd slapped her.

"Paxton, I would have called or emailed. Hell, I would have messaged you if anything had come up. We've talked about meeting for months. I wouldn't–"

Call it insanity or whatever you will, I did the only thing my brain could process at the time and took the one step toward her. Standing toe-to-toe, I let go of her arms, grabbed her face and crashed my lips to hers in an effort to shut her up. What was most surprising was how natural the act felt.

Her hand flew to her mouth as soon as I pulled back, eyes wide. No big surprise that I hadn't been the only one shocked at my actions.

Where had this sudden forwardness come from? Maybe it had been the relief that she was finally standing before me in person. Maybe it was that she'd proved, with her flustered rambling, that I hadn't been the only one looking forward our meeting.

Yes, things had gotten personal with our countless chats. But despite the numerous times we had flirted, exchanged photos, talked dirty, and even discussed how she had come up with some of the steamy scenes from her stories, I worried that I had crossed a line.

Even when this feels completely natural.

"Alissa, I'm–"

She shook her head and lifted her hand. "I knew that was coming at one point or another. I just didn't expect…" With a small upward quirk of her lips, she waved her hand in a dismissive gesture. "Never mind. That was nice."

I instantly breathed easier and grabbed her carry-on luggage. "Let's get out of here." I offered her my hand to hold. "Assuming you're still up for it, after my mauling you and all."

She giggled nervously but grasped my proffered grip in hers. I walked us out of luggage claim toward the parking structure with a certainty that I hadn't screwed things up so quick out of the gate, but maintained a level of wariness nonetheless.

W ith her luggage stowed in the back of my SUV, I headed to open the passenger side door for her.

If I'm going to be honest, my mind was presently stuck on our brief kiss.

Apparently I wasn't the only one.

Before I knew what hit me, Alissa had me pinned against the side of my vehicle, her body and lips smashed against mine.

My hands reached for her hips, pulling her into me as I licked her bottom lip, begging for entrance. The small taste of her in luggage claim had proven one thing—that I wanted more and as long as she was handing out samples, I wasn't going to decline her offer.

With a light moan, she granted me access while her hands found their way around my neck and into my hair. We breathed each other in.

Alissa pulled away first, her chest heaving for air. I was none the better. The woman knew how to kiss. So much so that a certain part of my anatomy had begun to stir with that more thorough taste of her.

Don't judge, it's been a while.

She hid her face in my chest.

I pecked the top of her head. "I guess we're even, huh?" She groaned, making me chuckle. I grabbed her chin, tilting it to reveal a beautiful crimson. A chaste press of my lips to hers seemed to alleviate her sudden embarrassment. "Let's get going." But that flush of colour in her cheeks was so becoming I simply had to tease her. "I can't have you all over me for everyone to see." I winked. Her blush had barely begun to fade as my words caused it to flare up once more, gaining me the reaction I was looking for. "I love that look on you by the way."

She waited for me to get behind the wheel before asking, "What look?"

"Your blush," I said and buckled myself in. "I know you told me about it but it's nothing like I had pictured. You're gorgeous."

She clasped her cheeks with her hands in an effort to conceal another wave of red and failing miserably. "You need to stop that."

In a mocked tone of innocence I said, "What?" I leaned over the middle console to flick her nose with an index finger. "It's true."

A soft laugh escaped her and she nodded toward the steering wheel. "Get to driving, will you?"

I dropped her luggage as soon as we crossed the threshold. Kicking the door shut, I pulled Alissa so her back was against my chest and hugged her from behind, setting my chin on her shoulder and savoring the feel of her against me.

A perfect fit.

"I can't believe you're actually here. You hungry?" It was nearly dinnertime and although I'd had a late lunch, my stomach grumbled.

She giggled at the noise. "A little." She wrapped her arms over mine. "What do you have in mind?"

I'm no culinary savant or anything, but I'm not the type of person to cook until I set fire to my kitchen either.

Until tonight apparently.

Part of it was Alissa's fault, despite the fact that she would beg to differ.

With a faltering grip, white powder filled the room after she recommended I use either cornstarch or flour to thicken the gravy. Flour, as it turns out, was all I had.

A fit of laughter consumed us as we attempted to clean up, making more of a mess out of ourselves than anything else.

She proceeded to wipe at me with a damp tea towel. When she got a little too close to a certain area, I grabbed her wrist to stop her. I pulled the cloth from her grip and wiped at her face while I felt her cool fingers wiping at mine.

Our eyes connected and locked.

Our laughter subsided.

The braised pork chops and boiling potatoes forgotten, we found ourselves wrapped in each other like a pair of randy teenagers. There was no telling who had started it. The chemistry was instantaneous.

When we came up for air, Alissa said, "Is it me or is it getting hot in here?"

As soon as she'd said it, something captured my attention from the corner of my eye, making me turn to look.

Our indulgence had resulted in the potatoes becoming an over-boiled pile of mush. The braised chops were charred, as the pan had caught fire. And the gravy did thicken—to the consistency of a dried up hockey puck stuck to the bottom of its pot.

Suffice it to say, dinner was effectively ruined.

Alissa was giggling into my back as I managed to put a stop to the tiny blaze with the help of a box of baking soda and an expired kitchen fire extinguisher.

Taking a deep breath, and looking over my shoulder at the woman still trying to gain her composure I asked her, "How do you feel about take-out?"

"I think it's a safer bet."

CHAPTER 2

Whed the kitchen was tidied up, the pots having been left to soak in the sink, and our food ordered, I offered Alissa a shower.

"You go ahead," she said. "I'll take mine after."

"I've got two bathrooms. You can use the one in my room since this is where you'll be staying. I'll take–"

"I can't kick you out," she said. "I could–"

"I didn't want to assume anything and I wanted you to be comfortable. The spare room doesn't have a bed yet, so I'll take the pullout couch. It's fine." I nodded toward the en suite bathroom. "Go ahead, it's through there. I'll take the main bath down the hall."

In a rush to get cleaned up and return to Alissa, I was fresh out of the shower when I realized that I hadn't grabbed any clean clothes to change into.

I wrapped the towel around my waist and headed out to gather something to put on.

Just as I slipped into my room, hoping to make a quick exit without being caught, I was graced with a sight that made my heart stop and start up again at a staccato pace.

Bent over, rummaging through her bag for what I

presumed was a shirt, Alissa's heart shaped ass, covered in a tight pair of blue jeans, was facing me along with her blonde locks dripping down her back.

I took a step forward and hadn't expected the floorboards to creak, giving my presence away.

She stood up ramrod straight and whirled around to face me, grabbing the first thing out of her bag to cover herself with.

I looked at it and burst out laughing. "You might need something more than that, sweetheart."

Her eyes looked down in horror when she found herself clutching a black lace bra. Blushing, her mouth opened as if to say something but nothing came out. Instead, I saw her gaze moving up my towel-clad torso, to my chest, her head tilting to the side, eyes widening, and her breathing picked up.

Grabbing her discarded towel, she quickly covered up and said, "I think I'm just going to—" She started to make a quick dash for the hallway with a mortified look on her face.

My hand clasped her arm to stop her. "Let me just grab the few things I didn't earlier and get out of here."

Turning away from her, I searched through my closet and pulled the few items I needed and headed for the exit. "I'll see you when you're done." I paused at the bedroom door before leaving her. "Has anyone ever told you that you're hot when you're flustered?"

I didn't wait for a response. A few steps down the hall, I could hear the woman grumbling to herself and smiled. Things were definitely far from boring with Alissa around.

The pizza arrived while Alissa was still getting herself straightened out. I figured that she was done by now but that she was dealing with some residual embarrassment before coming downstairs to join me. In the short amount of time

since her arrival, I had come to think of her meek demeanor

as a rather endearing quality of hers.

I poured some wine for us after getting the plates ready, knowing that she wouldn't be that much longer.

I smiled as I replayed the earlier series of events in my head.

Like any normal hot-blooded male out there, I'd be crazy if I said I didn't want to get laid by the woman currently holed up in my bedroom. We had chemistry, there was no denying that, but the gentleman in me urged me to slow things down a bit. There was something greater to lose here; a friendship that I wasn't willing to part with.

And maybe something greater?

The couch dipped beside me and the wine in my goblet sloshed about, bringing me back to the present.

"So, I guess you didn't lie when you said you knew how to make a towel look good, huh?" She smirked.

I eyed her amused face, surprised at her overtness and humored all the same. "I deserve that. I'm sorry for barging in. I–"

She placed a hand on my arm and squeezed lightly. "It's okay. You just took me by surprise."

"Here." I handed over her glass of wine, watching as she took a large gulp of the Cabernet Sauvignon. Trying to get my head back in the game had proved useless with my next statement. "For what it's worth, those jeans look fantastic but I have to confess that my imagination is running wild with pictures of you wearing that black lace bra you were holding on to."

She laughed. "Boy, you're a cheeky one, aren't you?"

I smiled, happy that our familiar playful banter from our online conversations had begun to creep into our face-to-face setting as time went on. I was starting to see more of the Alissa I had grown to know over the last ten months. Witnessing a genuine physical reaction instead of those stupid emoticon faces or some video rendition of her was a refreshing change. I was able to read her like one of her books, and what I took in only made me want to be around her more. There was a level of comfort between us that I hadn't seen coming, despite our few moments of awkwardness.

After dinner, I noticed Alissa fighting off the urge to fall asleep as our movie went on, so I pulled her legs on top of my lap in order to let her stretch out and be more comfortable.

When the credits began to roll, I turned the TV off and lifted the sleeping woman into my arms. By instinct, her arms wrapped themselves around my neck. Nuzzling against my jaw, Alissa mumbled something indiscernible while I carried her to my bedroom.

I set her down on my bed and tried to pull back but she woke and latched onto my shirt, capturing me with those cerulean eyes of hers.

I froze.

"Please don't go," she whispered and pulled me down. I had to brace myself to prevent from toppling over and crushing her.

Butterflies fluttered about in my stomach. "Are you sure?"

She bit down on her lower lip, making me wish that I could nibble it myself. That simple innocent action of hers had been driving me crazy every time she'd done it.

I felt her fingers around the belt loops to my jeans, forcing me lower.

Her lips brushed against mine. "This is your house, it's a big bed, and you're not sleeping on the couch."

I played with her hair and studied her. "It's not so bad."

"Pax?" Her gaze flittered between my mouth and eyes.

"Hmm?" I leaned toward her.

"Kiss—"

I never let her finish, knowing that we both wanted the

same thing.

She ran her hands from my belt loops to around my hips and under my shirt. The feather-like contact as her fingers traced about my lower back heated my flesh. She nibbled on my lip. Her soft tongue met mine as we sought closeness. She tasted sweet and I wondered what the rest of her would taste like, or if I'd be lucky enough to find out. Something told me that I was well on my way with the way things were heating up.

I let my hand wander from her side down to her hip. Her leg folded up at the knee, allowing me better access to squeeze her jean-clad cheek, causing her to moan into my mouth. I kissed the length of her jaw, down to the side of her neck, up to her ear.

"You have no idea how much I want you right now," I said.

Her body trembled.

I nipped her lobe, eliciting a whimper from her as her hands came free of my shirt and made their way to my hair. I felt the prickling of my scalp followed by a rush of arousal as she pulled.

My pants tightened further. If she had any question as to how much she turned me on, the vixen that lay beneath me had a feasible answer as I pressed my lower half into hers.

Alissa rolled us over and straddled my waist with a wry grin. "If you want something, Paxton, you've got to take it." She grabbed onto the hem of my shirt and I arched my back to help her remove it.

A look of hunger twinkled in her eyes as she studied my upper body. A finger ran up the middle of my stomach, starting at the waist of my jeans, circling my navel. The tickling digit changed to an open palm, which rubbed my chest as she leaned forward to bring her lips inches from mine.

I reveled in all things Alissa.

The woman was a temptress, a master at seduction, and she behaved as if she had no clue to her prowess. That hot and moist tongue of hers, mixed with her nips and the series of open-mouthed kisses heading down my torso, was wreaking havoc on my senses. An internal fight broke out between my urge to flip her over and exact my sensual revenge, and that of staying put to see where she was going to end up next.

Reduced to breathlessness, I managed, "Allie?"

Her fingers toyed with the button at the top of my jeans. Her mouth latched onto one of my nipples, flicking that wicked tongue of hers over the hardened disk. "Hmm?" The vibrations sent electrical currents throughout my body.

She leaned up to kiss my mouth. I felt her smile against my lips and saw the crinkling at her eyes when the button snapped out of its eyelet.

In that moment, something snapped in me also.

I flipped us over, grabbed her hands and pinned them above her head with one of mine. My other hand roamed free to find the exposed flesh around her stomach from her shirt riding up.

"Too many layers." I grunted my disapproval.

She helped me with stripping her shirt, and discarded it to the floor much like mine had been. I looked upon her as her blonde hair draped over my pillow, garnishing her head as if it were a halo. She looked delicious, and I was desperate to taste more than just her mouth.

"So soft," I said against the middle of her stomach while depositing soft kisses on my way up to those lace-covered mounds of hers.

I slid my hand underneath the band and took a breast in my hand, pinching its nipple and rolling it. She gasped and arched toward me.

Junior swelled to desperation in my jeans. I knew I'd have to at least unzip myself to allow for a bit of breathing room, and soon.

I pulled myself off of her and kneeled between her legs. Her face was flushed, her breathing was labored and her

eyes… *Wow!* They were the brightest deep blue I had ever seen.

My hands reached for her fly and button. She tilted her hips up in permission and I pulled her denims off.

Damn! The woman sure knew her lingerie.

I grunted my approval at the sight of the matching black lace accentuating her slender, toned legs, and looking forward to the time they would be wrapped around me.

Amusement could be seen all over her face as she observed me taking her in.

"You look like a kid who's visiting an amusement park for the first time." Her voice had turned husky. "Your turn. Take off those pants, stud."

I mock saluted, gaining me a giggle while I proceeded to stand beside the bed and dropped *trou.*

Feeling her urge to stay close, she knelt on the edge of the mattress. Her palms met my chest; leaving a burning trail from the moment they made contact. Our eyes met and all playfulness, all mischievousness, was absent. In its stead, vulnerability dominated.

In that moment, I was reminded of Alissa's past relationship troubles. She knew of my hang-ups as much as I knew about hers. Honestly, she'd been the one to make me see that there was more to life than just existing. That there was someone out there that was better suited for me than my ex-wife ever had been.

Julie.

Talk about a proverbial bucket of iced water to cool things down a notch.

I need to tell her.

Here she was, single, hot and ready and even though she knew of my separation, I felt like a cheat.

A moron.

A liar.

Yeah, definitely a lying cheat of a moron.